"What are you doing?"

Rachel pulled her arm away from the stranger.

"We need to talk." He gestured up the road. "Somewhere quieter." His loose trench coat shifted, showing a holster beneath. "Please, Nora."

"My name is Rachel, and I have no idea what you're– Is that a gun?" Raw fear tightened her voice to a squeak.

The man raised his eyebrows. "Standard equipment for a US marshal."

Rachel blinked. "You are a marshal?"

The man stared at her. Rachel could see the pupils of his eyes widen. "You really *don't* know who I am."

"No."

Rachel had the strangest feeling that by saying this one word she had hurt him. If so, he recovered quickly. "Your guard dogs are coming. Why do they always follow you around? I need more information, but I don't want to talk to you in front of strangers. Something is wrong here."

Evelyn M. Hill loves to spend time traveling around the Pacific Northwest, which is filled with settings that inspire her romantic suspense and historical novels. When she's not writing, you can usually find her attempting to garden, surprising her family with "adventurous" meals (not their description), or trying to persuade the cat and the dog to grasp the concept of peaceful coexistence. You can visit her at her website, evelynhillauthor.com.

Books by Evelyn M. Hill

Love Inspired Suspense

Dangerous Deception

Love Inspired Historical

His Forgotten Fiancée

DANGEROUS DECEPTION

EVELYN M. HILL

LOVE INSPIRED SUSPENSE
INSPIRATIONAL ROMANCE

LOVE INSPIRED® SUSPENSE
INSPIRATIONAL ROMANCE

ISBN-13: 978-1-335-72208-9

Dangerous Deception

Copyright © 2020 by Mary E.B. Carson

Love Inspired
22 Adelaide St. West, 40th Floor
Toronto, Ontario M5H 4E3, Canada
www.Harlequin.com

Printed in U.S.A.

And he said unto me, My grace is sufficient for thee:
for my strength is made perfect in weakness.
Most gladly therefore will I rather glory in my infirmities,
that the power of Christ may rest upon me.
—*2 Corinthians* 12:9

To my mother, who always told me I should write a book

ONE

The stranger was trouble. Rachel knew that the moment she saw him.

The tall man stood across the street from the café in a confident stance, his open trench coat fluttering in the breeze off the Oregon coast, hands in his trouser pockets. He paid no attention to the other residents of the tiny town of Sleepy Cove as they passed by. His gaze never wavered from his target: Rachel.

At the sight of that strange man staring at her, all her vague fears crystallized into solid reality.

"I think he's a talent scout looking for the latest movie star," elderly Miss Trant said. When she'd held the job of postmistress, she'd gotten to look at all the celebrity magazines first, and it definitely affected her worldview.

Mrs. Benson, who used to run the county library before she retired, eyed the man with distinct approval. "He's handsome enough to be in the movies himself. That dark hair is a bit shaggy to my way of thinking, and he could use a shave, but there's no denying he's easy on the eyes. Maybe he fancies our Rachel."

The way a hawk fancies a mouse, perhaps.

The stranger's attention never shifted from Rachel. Those light eyes pierced straight through to her soul. Just looking at him made her pulse spike.

Rachel refilled Mrs. Benson's cup of coffee and went back to prepping for the lunch crowd. The morning rush had ended, and the two elderly ladies were the only customers in the Blue Whale Café at the moment.

As she worked, Rachel gave herself orders, as if her hands belonged to a stranger. That was easier, somehow.

Roll up the cutlery in the napkin. Lay the bundle aside with the rest. Take another napkin and roll the cutlery up. Keep acting as if everything is all right. It's just your imagination playing tricks on you.

Her imagination did play tricks on her. Rachel knew that. She had wrecked her car one night, on a winding road in the hills, and ended up in the hospital in Sleepy Cove to recover. That was when the nightmares had started.

And the anxiety attacks. And the nagging sense that something was wrong.

If her friends discovered how unreal her life seemed at times, they would be convinced that Rachel was losing her mind. She'd be shut up in an institution. For her own good, of course, and out of love rather than malice.

Which somehow made it all the worse.

Someone nudged her hand, and Rachel reacted instinctively, jerking away from the touch and clenching her hands into fists.

Mrs. Benson drew back. "Are you all right, Rachel? I was wondering if you could get me a slice of the key lime pie, dear?"

"Of course." Rachel forced herself to laugh off her reaction. Time to change the subject. "Mrs. Benson, aren't you a happily married woman? You shouldn't be ogling strange young men."

"For forty-five years now, and that doesn't mean my eyes aren't working just fine."

"I've never read a single scientific paper that posited a correlation between a happy marriage and its effect on eyesight." Rachel slid the pie slice across the counter.

Corrie wandered over to the counter, pushing her thick black frame glasses back up her nose. In her soft-spoken drawl, she said, "Rachel, dear, I'm sorry to be a bother, but have you taken your medication today? You know you forgot the other day."

The gentle nagging was so familiar it was almost comforting. Rachel gave her usual half-joking protest. "Corrie, you're my boss, not my mother."

"My dear, by the time you get to my age, you learn to take care of your health."

"Oh, please." Mrs. Benson lowered her fork, shaking her head. "You're both children."

Corrie poured a glass of water and watched Rachel swallow her pills. "The doctor said these are exactly what you need right now."

Rachel had no secrets from Corrie. After the accident, Corrie had taken her in, let her stay until she was well enough to hold down a job and then found her work in the café. Still raw from the loss of her parents, Rachel had been grateful for Corrie always wanting to make sure she was all right. So she put down the empty glass and forced herself to smile at Corrie. "I know. Dr. Green said it would take time for all the issues from the car crash to clear up."

"You poor dear," Mrs. Benson said. "At least the scars on your face don't show anymore. Corrie, I've had an idea. What if you painted the walls a different color? Something brighter, to attract the tourists in for a nice meal."

"Or perhaps a nice wallpaper?" Miss Trant leaned her elbows on the counter, settling in for a long discussion. "I've seen some lovely designs when I was looking through the magazines at the grocery store."

"It would be too much trouble to change things," Corrie said, as she always did. "Besides, I'm putting all my money into investments. One day, it'll pay off. Then I'll be off to Hawaii. Or maybe Florida. Somewhere I can have my own beachfront condo." Her voice turned dreamy. "I want to live in a place where it's warm even when it rains."

Rachel stopped paying attention. Another perfectly normal day at work. Everything was the way it should be.

Almost.

Her gaze went back across the street as if drawn there by a magnet. She went to put the pie back above the counter. Surely, by the time she faced the window again, the man would have directed his attention elsewhere.

No. When she turned back, he was in the exact same position.

The man would *not* stop staring at Rachel. It bothered her. A lot. But then these days she was constantly fighting off the sense that something was dreadfully wrong.

Lord, what is wrong with me? Why am I always afraid? There's no reason for it.

It was as if she were operating on two levels at the same time: the sane, everyday world and a sinister landscape of midnight shadows. The only thing she could do was cling to her faith and keep on as if everything were normal. Because of course it was.

There.

Was.

Nothing.

Wrong.

On impulse, Rachel untied her apron. "I'm tired of standing here, being stared at. I'm going to go ask him what he wants."

Corrie's glasses had slid halfway down her nose again. She pushed them back up. "I don't think that's a good idea," she scolded, in her usual gentle manner. "You're too trusting, Rachel. That's going to get you into trouble one of these days. For all you know, that man might be dangerous. Get Tony to talk to him."

Rachel folded up the apron and left it on a stool. "No. This guy is starting to get on my nerves."

If she confronted this man, it would be

standing up to everything that scared her. Now, before she could lose her nerve. In the middle of Main Street, with people all around.

"I really think you should wait. Give the medication time to take effect. Then you'll be sure not to get an anxiety attack. Besides, you need to take care of our customers. I have to go into the back room to make a phone call."

"I was thinking that I might like a little something to go with my coffee," Miss Trant said. "Rachel, dear, is there any of that apple pie left?"

"I'll get it." Corrie fetched the pie and placed it on the counter. "Now, if you ladies will excuse me for a moment?"

"Off to phone a boyfriend?" Mrs. Benson said slyly.

"Better than that," Corrie retorted. "Off to phone my financial advisor." As she turned away, her sleeve caught on the pie pan, dragging it off the counter. The pie landed on the floor at Rachel's feet. Pie-side down, of course. Corrie sighed. "And I just took that out of the oven."

"On second thought, maybe a slice of that key lime pie would be better," Miss Trant said.

"I'll deal with it," Rachel said. She served

Miss Trant her pie and then fetched the dust-
pan and knelt down to clean up the mess.

As Corrie went into the back room and shut
the door behind her, Rachel emptied the pie
into the garbage. Then she came back to the
counter. "Do you think you ladies would be all
right if I step away for a moment?" She already
knew the answer. The two women practically
lived at the café, to the point where Corrie had
trouble shooing them out when she closed in
the afternoon.

"Oh, Helena and I will be just fine. Don't
worry about us," Mrs. Benson assured her.
Miss Trant nodded.

"I'll be right back," Rachel said. Without
giving herself time for second thoughts, she
slipped out through the front door. She had
to confront this man now, before she lost her
nerve.

The stranger did not move as she approached. Close up, she noticed the dark stubble covering that hard jaw. His lean face could
have been carved out of granite, but underneath the imperturbable facade, she sensed an
anger banked down low, waiting for its chance
to flare up.

The man's eyes were a clear light blue, in
startling contrast to his tanned face. Some-

thing about those light eyes teased her like a song she could almost recall. But she had no time to pin down who exactly he reminded her of. She had more immediate problems. For no reason that Rachel could see, he looked absolutely furious—with her.

"I thought so," he said. His voice was low, but she caught the words clearly. "I wasn't certain, not at first, but—your eyes. *They* haven't changed." His eyes narrowed. "Do you intend to give me an explanation at some point?"

Rachel felt a tug, an urge to take a step closer, and yet she knew she was already dancing on the knife-edge of danger just being as close as she was to him. "Why do you keep staring at me? What do you want?"

"There's an old saying." The stranger leaned against the wall and folded his arms. "Keep your friends close and your enemies closer."

"And which are you?"

"You tell me."

The stranger's gaze never left Rachel's face. She was pinned down by it like a specimen under a microscope. "I don't even know who you are."

"Of course you don't."

The lazy, mocking tone sparked an anger that warmed her veins, burning away the fear for a moment. Rachel took a step forward. "Look. I don't know what kind of game this is, but—"

"Hey, Rach!" Tony's voice boomed out and Rachel jumped back. For such a little man, the local sheriff had a voice that could rattle windows. His pudgy, sunburned face was creased with concern. "What are you doing out here?"

Corrie ran across the street, her glasses slipping down to the tip of her nose. "There you are!" She pulled Rachel away from the stranger, her fingers digging into Rachel's arm. "I thought you'd gone into the storage room. What are you doing out here? Is there a problem?"

"That's what I was wondering." Tony stepped between Rachel and the stranger. "You have something to say?" The stranger's eyes narrowed as he surveyed the sheriff, but he did not reply. "Well then, I'd say we're done here." Tony took Rachel's other arm and guided her back to the café.

Rachel couldn't help but feel like a wayward child being hauled home by her parents. That was absurd, of course. It was good of them to worry about her.

Tony opened the door and stood aside to let Corrie and Rachel enter. "Rach, what were you thinking? You know how anxious you get in new situations."

Rachel picked up her apron and tied it around her waist. "I needed to find out what the man wanted."

"By yourself?" Tony shook his head. "You need to be more careful. Remember how scared you were when you first came to town? You used to jump at the slightest sound. You're better now, but still. You should try to avoid stress, keep quiet, play it safe."

"Corrie was right across the street." Even to her own ears, Rachel sounded defensive. She liked Tony, but sometimes it rankled when he treated her as if she were an invalid. "I knew it would be safe. And I couldn't—" She stopped, took a breath. "I couldn't just sit here like a frightened rabbit. I'm tired of being afraid all the time."

"You shouldn't have gone over there." Corrie ran her hand through her hair, knocking her hairnet askew and making her curls tumble around her face. "I don't like the looks of that man. These days, you never can tell."

"I'm sorry I worried you," Rachel said meekly. "I know you are only trying to help me. I'll be more careful next time."

The frown line between Corrie's eyebrows relaxed. "That's all right, then."

Adjusting her hairnet, Corrie went back to serving coffee, while Rachel moved behind the counter and began to assemble Tony's lunch-time sandwich. She didn't bother to ask what he wanted; Tony invariably ordered the same thing. He liked his routine, safe and predictable. As Corrie did.

As she worked, Rachel couldn't help going over every detail of her conversation with the strange man, analyzing every gesture, every word. Why was he fixated on her? She snuck a glance back over her shoulder, but the sidewalk across the street was empty.

One by one, the lunch crowd began to trickle in. For once, keeping busy did not help. Rachel rubbed the back of her neck, but the tension in her muscles did not ease.

Tony came up to the register to pay his bill. "I don't like to see you unhappy, Rach. If you feel anxious, you should call Doc Green. See if she can fit you in. I know those therapy sessions do you a world of good."

"That's a sweet thought, Tony. But I really don't think—"

"I'll walk you over. I'm sure Corrie would let you off early."

"Oh, no, I couldn't possibly—"

But Tony had already raised his voice to call down the counter. "Hey, Cor! Mind if Rach takes off early today? She's feeling poorly."

Corrie shook her head, which made her brown-gray curls slip out of her hairnet. She tucked her hair back in. "No, I don't mind. You go on, Rachel."

Rachel gave in. They were right; the therapy sessions helped with her anxiety issues. And she trusted Dr. Green, truly she did. It was just that the sight of any doctor brought back flashbacks to her arrival in Sleepy Cove.

Night after night, Rachel would dream of being taken away in the middle of the night, men in white coats grabbing her. She could never recall the exact details, but the surroundings never changed—white walls, stainless steel tables and an overwhelming sense of despair.

When she had been released from the hospital, Rachel formed an absolute resolution that she was never going back. The money from the insurance company had covered her expenses until she was able to go back to work. She had taken a job at the café with Corrie and started going to Dr. Green three times a week to help deal with her anxieties. Dr. Green assured Rachel she was getting better.

Even so, sometimes Rachel would wake up in her little apartment in a cold sweat. And for a moment, the everyday objects around her would look strange, foreign. Then something in the back of her mind would shift and everything would be safe and familiar again.

She should be ashamed of herself for dreading doctor visits. She owed everything to Dr. Green. The woman had gone out of her way to help Rachel, finding a place for her to stay with Corrie and encouraging Rachel to take a job at the café. "It will help you deal with your anxieties to have a steady job," she'd said. And she was right. Working at the café had introduced Rachel to the people in the town and helped her feel as if she were settling in. Everyone had been very kind. She should be grateful. No, she *would* feel grateful. She just had to keep reminding herself to practice gratitude.

Tony escorted her to the doctor's office, a little converted cottage a block off from Main Street. Even in winter, flowers grew in the front yard—showy scarlet camellias and fragrant white winter jasmine. Pink roses twined around the posts on the porch, their sweet scent overpowering her anxieties, enforcing peace.

Dr. Green came out onto the porch to greet them, slipping a voice recorder into the pocket of her white doctor's coat. With her thin wire glasses and her dark hair slicked into a neat bun, she always reminded Rachel of the epitome of a cool, detached scientist. Her deep brown eyes crinkled as she gave Rachel a smile. "Yes, of course, I can fit you in for a session. Go lie down in the therapy room. I'll be right with you after I finish updating my records." She disappeared into her office.

Tony patted Rachel on the shoulder. "I'll just wait right here until you're finished, walk you back to your apartment. That way, you'll feel safe." Even as he spoke, though, his eyes traveled up to the shop on the corner.

Tony was always so concerned with making sure she didn't have an anxiety attack. He hovered over her like a mother hen. Sometimes, Rachel had the uneasy feeling that he wanted more than friendship from her. Since Tony never came out and said anything, Rachel was spared the awkward situation of explaining that she didn't think of him that way. She wasn't sure what her type was, but it definitely wasn't Tony.

Instead, Rachel always tried to keep things on a playful level. She gave him a light push.

"Go on. I heard that Sal's Sweets has got a new saltwater taffy flavor."

"Hmm." Tony kept a straight face, but the twinkle in his eyes belied his serious tone. "I should investigate that rumor, see if it's true. I'll come back later to walk you home."

But when Rachel came out of the doctor's cottage, Tony was nowhere in sight. Rachel felt relieved. Then she felt guilty. She shouldn't be so ungrateful.

Dr. Green followed her out onto the front porch. She touched Rachel on the arm, and Rachel jumped back without thinking. Dr. Green frowned. "Maybe we should increase your sessions to four times a week."

Rachel hesitated. She did not want to hurt the doctor's feelings. Nevertheless, she had to say, "I've been going to you three times a week for months. If the therapy is really helping, not just making me feel better temporarily, shouldn't I be needing to come to you less?"

Dr. Green patted her on the shoulder. "Rachel, I hear what you're saying. But trust me to decide what's best for you."

The words were kindly meant. It was wrong of Rachel to find Dr. Green's tone condescending. It was wrong for Rachel to want to prove that she was in control of her own life. Dr. Green was only trying to help her.

Even so, Rachel couldn't completely suppress the flare of resentment. She ducked her head to hide her expression and put one hand on the railing at the head of the stairs.

Dr. Green went on, "I don't think you realize how important this treatment is to your overall health. It's not too strong a statement to say that it is saving your life. These pills help you deal with your anxieties and delusions. Truly, I think if you weren't on this medication, we'd have to resort to more drastic measures to deal with your problems."

Rachel's hand clenched around the bannister in a death grip.

Breathe.

Another breath. In and out.

Again.

Don't let the fear show.

Rachel forced herself to look up. Dr. Green was watching her intently. Rachel had no doubt the other woman noticed every twitch of expression on her face. Nevertheless, Rachel forced her words out past suddenly dry lips. "You mean I'd be in an institution."

"You don't need to worry, Rachel. I only

want what's best for you. You trust me, don't you?"

"Of course." The words came automatically, without conscious thought. But that didn't lessen the fear that threatened to drown Rachel.

"Then I'll schedule you for another appointment tomorrow." Dr. Green looked around. "Where is Tony? I thought he was going to walk back with you. You need someone to escort you. I heard about that odd man who was bothering you earlier."

"Who told you about that?" Not that Rachel cared, but anything was better than talking about hospitalization.

"Oh, I think Miss Trant must have mentioned it. Or maybe it was Mrs. Benson. You know she likes to share everything that goes on in town. But you need to be more careful. You're at a sensitive stage in your recovery. You need to be around cheerful, positive people. You don't want to spend time around negative people, who could influence your thinking down the wrong path."

The doctor probably meant to reassure Rachel, but instead her words bit into her nerves like barbed hooks, shredding the last wisps of peace she'd felt after the therapy session.

"I don't think the man wanted to harm me. I have to say, the idea of anything bad happening to me in Sleepy Cove seems absurd." *It's the world outside that terrifies me.*

Dr. Green took off her glasses and rubbed them against her white lab coat. "These days, you can't be too trusting. Not even in a place like Sleepy Cove. Where *is* Tony?"

"He likes to stop at that saltwater taffy shop on the corner." Rachel clasped her hands together, gripping tightly. "That's just a few stores down from here. I can walk up there by myself. Wouldn't that be safe?"

Her pleading seemed to please Dr. Green. "I suppose that would be all right. Everything will be fine, dear. So long as you trust me to do what's best for you."

The doctor went back into the cottage and Rachel escaped. As she turned on Main Street, she darted a glance inside the sweet shop. Sure enough, Tony was there, bending over the counter, looking at the selection.

Rachel hurried past, not slowing until she was well down the block. There was no harm in walking along the street by herself. She had to find a way to conquer her fears and get better. She *had* to.

The therapy sessions had always eased the

sense that something was wrong with her. Lately, though, that feeling of peace and security had not been lasting as long as it used to. Inevitably, the dread crept back, like the fog that lay offshore, waiting to surround her, to cling like a second skin, pressing down until it felt hard to breathe.

Rachel shook herself out of her dark thoughts. *Think of all the many things you should be grateful for.* Starting with where she lived. Sleepy Cove was tucked between the hills of the Coast Range and the Pacific Ocean. Fog gathered on the horizon, but overhead the sun shone bright in a cloudless blue sky. She'd found a place where people liked her and she liked them. And it was a beautiful place to live. Idyllic. Main Street looked picture-postcard perfect, lined with old Victorian houses and storefronts with neat white trim. Tourists came from Portland and Seattle just to stay for a week or two, and Rachel got to live there year-round.

She turned down the alley that was a shortcut to her tiny attic apartment above Corrie's house. The tall buildings on either side blocked out the sun, leaving the alley in shade. In the narrowed space, the sound of her shoes hitting the pavement was magnified, distorted into echoes. Then she heard the sound of heavier footsteps behind her.

A quick glance over her shoulder showed a man silhouetted in the entrance to the alley, his face hidden in shadow.

Anxiety seized her in a viselike grip, tightening her diaphragm and making it hard to breathe. The alley was isolated. No one would hear her if she called for help.

Rachel picked up her pace. The rhythm of footsteps increased in tempo. The man was close behind her now.

She'd never make it up the steps to her apartment in time. So she bypassed the stairs and went straight for the highway at the end of the alley and the safety of being around other people. It was a busy street, with tourists driving through town at highway speeds. She was more likely to find other people there.

Rachel burst out of the alley almost at a run. She looked over her shoulder again, still moving forward. Then she stumbled, almost falling into the street before getting her balance again.

"Watch out." A hand gripped her shoulder, pulling her back from the curb. A car flashed past, missing her by inches. She heard the strange man's deep voice, close to her ear.

"Some people drive through here like they're still on the freeway."

Rachel twisted around to face him. Her heart was still racing, but she felt better now that she was out of the narrow confines of the alley. All the same, she took a few paces back, putting some sidewalk between herself and the stranger. He held his hands up. "Sorry if I startled you."

"If you don't want to startle me, I suggest you stop stalking me."

"I wasn't *stalking* you."

Rachel crossed her arms.

"I just wanted to talk to you without your friends interrupting."

"What is so important that you have to follow me around town like this?"

"I just want to know why. I need to understand. Then I'll leave you alone, if that's really what you want from me."

The man's expression gave nothing away, but Rachel detected a hint of emotion with that last sentence. He almost sounded…sad? That couldn't be right. All the same, she was curious. "What do you want to know?"

"Why you left."

Rachel shook her head. "You're not making any sense." Out of the corner of her eye, she caught a flash of bright color. She turned her head.

A child darted across the road, pink jacket and flying blond hair. She was halfway across before a car horn blared. A red convertible was coming down the road fast. The child froze, hands going to her mouth in horror.

The stranger moved fast, tackling the child and rolling with her to the curb as the driver slammed on his brakes in a shriek of metal.

The car passed them, skidding to the side of the road. Then there was stillness.

The stranger sat up, brushing dirt off the little girl. "Are you all right?"

The girl lay there, looking up at him. She wrinkled her forehead, as if not sure whether to cry or not. Rachel knelt down beside him, her focus on the child. She touched her head with gentle fingers. "Lie still a moment. I'm sorry. I know it's cold on the ground." She patted her pockets and turned to the stranger. "Do you have a phone? I need a flashlight."

Without a word, the stranger flicked on the flashlight on his phone and handed it to her. Rachel directed the light into the child's eyes, first one, then the other.

The driver came up, red-faced and worried,

trying to cover his embarrassment with bluster. "I never came near her."

"No thanks to your driving." Rachel's gaze never wavered from the child's face, checking her reactions, but her voice was sharp and decisive as she addressed the man. "You need to slow down and watch for pedestrians."

The stranger asked, "What are you doing?"

"Checking the pupil response," she said absently. "No sign of concussion."

The driver said hopefully, "Are you a doctor, ma'am?"

Rachel stared down at her hands as if she'd never seen them before. "I… Well, I just knew what to do."

The child's mother came running up, wide-eyed and flushed, babbling out thanks and recriminations and admonishments all together. She wrapped her arms around the little girl. She kissed the child over and over and smoothed down her tousled hair.

"I think she's going to be all right," Rachel told her. "The pupils are fine. But she did hit her head, so you need to get her checked out. I don't see any sign of concussion, but your own doctor will want to verify that."

The woman wrapped her arms around her

child, holding her close. "I'm just so thankful a doctor was here to help my little girl."

Rachel looked at her and blinked, as if coming to herself. She handed the phone back to the stranger. "No. No, I'm not a doctor."

The woman frowned in puzzlement. "Then why did you say *your own doctor* if you're not one?"

"I don't know why I said that." Rachel got up, hurriedly brushing dirt off her legs. "You need to take her to someone who knows what they're doing."

The woman started to thank Rachel again, but the stranger held up his hand. "If she's fine, we need to be on our way." He took Rachel by the elbow and guided her away. Behind them, the woman went back to berating the driver, who was still trying to excuse himself.

Rachel pulled her arm away from the stranger. "What are you doing?"

"We need to talk." He gestured up the road. "Somewhere quieter." His loose trench coat shifted, showing a holster beneath. "Please, Nora."

"My name is Rachel, and I have no idea what you're—is that a gun?" Raw fear tightened her voice to a squeak.

The man raised his eyebrows. "Standard equipment for a US marshal."

Rachel blinked. "You are a marshal?"

The man stared at her. "You really *don't* know who I am."

"No."

Rachel had the strangest feeling that by saying this one word she had hurt him. If so, he recovered quickly, extending a hand toward the walkway. "Please. Can we find someplace a little quieter? I'm sorry if I frightened you earlier. I didn't mean to upset you."

Oddly enough, Rachel discovered that she wasn't upset any longer. As she fell into step with him, strolling down the street, she tried to analyze her feelings. The more she talked with the man, the more she found herself relaxing, the tension in her muscles ebbing away. It was as if something in the back of her mind were whispering that she was safe around him, that he would protect her.

Then the man's attention got distracted. He looked across the street and frowned. "Your guard dogs are coming. Why do they always follow you around? I don't understand what's going on in this town, not yet. Be careful, Nora. Something is wrong here."

Before Rachel could reply, Tony ran up, with

a wide-eyed Corrie panting behind him. "Hey, what's going on?" He had his gun out.

Corrie reached past Tony and pulled Rachel away from the stranger. "I saw that man grab you." For a mild-mannered lady, she was giving the man an amazingly fierce glare.

The stranger belted his trench coat. "I just wanted to talk to the lady. No harm in talking. She looked like someone I used to know."

Surely if the man were a US marshal, wouldn't he identify himself to Tony? Had Rachel misunderstood him? If she were imagining things, the last thing she wanted to do was admit it. She said, "It was a misunderstanding."

"Yes," the stranger said. "Just a misunderstanding." He turned to Rachel. "I'm sorry if I made you feel uncomfortable." Polite, as if meeting her at a church social.

Rachel's cheeks heated. What a fool she must look right now. "Thank you."

Tony let his breath out in a frustrated huff of air and told the stranger, "She's not interested in talking to you."

The stranger's eyes flickered from Corrie to Tony. Rachel thought for a moment he was going to reply, but he merely nodded and turned away. Then he stopped, extending his hand toward Rachel. "Here. You dropped your cell phone while you were checking on the child."

As he handed her the phone, his fingertips brushed across her palm. The touch seemed to alert every nerve ending in her body. An extraordinary feeling, as if he had woken something inside her that she hadn't even known was there.

The stranger himself appeared unaffected. He turned away and walked down the street with long unhurried strides.

Tony looked her up and down. "You doing okay now, Rach?"

"Yes." She summoned up a shaky smile. "No problem." She wasn't sure if that were true, but there was no point in making Tony more protective.

Corrie frowned, a deep V appearing between her eyebrows. It made her look sharp and shrewish, not at all her usual apologetic manner. "Tony, I thought you were going to escort her home."

Before Tony could respond, Rachel put in, "I wanted to walk by myself for once."

"Now, you know how we worry about you, Rachel."

Tony put his gun away, but his hand twitched

toward it occasionally. "If that man bothers you again, Rach, you let me know."

"Thank you," Rachel said wearily. She appreciated that this was their way of showing they cared about her, but sometimes their protective nature felt like a burden too heavy to bear. It seemed easier to give in. "Right now, I just want to go home."

Corrie put her arm around Rachel. "Come to my place. I'll make you some chamomile tea. You know that always helps you to calm down."

Rachel allowed herself to be led away. The whole incident had taken only a minute or two. She could still feel the sensation of the stranger's fingertips brushing against her palm.

And she could not shake the memory of the look in his eyes when he realized she did not know him from Adam.

Michael Sullivan strode down the sidewalk, scanning the quiet town on every side. There weren't many tourists this time of year, though a few retirees pottered up and down, looking in the old-fashioned shops and Victorian houses. The whole place looked more like Mayberry than anything in real life. Innocent. Safe.

Deceptive.

He kept his hands in his pockets so no one could see them clenched into fists. He wanted to hit something. This might look like a typical small town, but something was very wrong here.

Nora had stood there so meekly, her hands clasped in front of her and her shoulders hunched. Her features had been altered subtly—a straighter nose, a slightly higher forehead. But it was more than the surgical alterations; almost everything about her had changed. With her hair pulled back in a severe ponytail and wearing a drab sweater and baggy jeans, she was a far cry from the stylish, confident woman he had last seen. He would have thought her a different woman altogether—except for one thing.

Michael had looked deep into Nora's eyes. He could never mistake those. They were a warm brown flecked with gold. Beautiful.

And they held not a shred of recognition in them.

He hadn't expected that. He had come prepared for a confrontation, an argument, an explanation. Michael needed to know why she had left, why she covered her tracks so completely and came to this tiny town. Why she had not left him even a note. But he had looked into her eyes and she had not known him. That threw him.

He didn't know what was going on here, and the uncertainty made him angry.

Once he got to his SUV, he climbed inside and slammed the door. He took a deep breath, centering himself.

Then he called his friend. Michael had met Greg Parker during his stint in the army. Once out of the military, Parker had settled in Portland, a few hours' drive from this small town Michael found himself in.

"Parker? What would make a woman lose her memory?" he asked without preamble.

"Hello to you, too, Sullivan," Parker replied. "I always had the impression women found you unforgettable. If you're losing your touch, you need a matchmaker, not a psychiatrist."

"Very amusing." Michael gripped his cell phone as though it would help him hold on to his patience, never his strong point. "I found Nora."

"Oh." The levity dropped from his friend's voice. "Is she all right?"

"No. I can say that with one hundred percent certainty. She doesn't have a clue who I am."

"Seriously? She's not pretending for some reason?"

"What do you mean by that?"

"Well…you had said you two argued before you went on that last mission."

"We had an argument. But Nora would never pretend not to know me. Something is wrong. She's cut her hair, she calls herself Rachel, works as a waitress and she's even had plastic surgery. But before you ask, yes. It's Nora." He plunged into details, describing the situation.

His friend listened in silence.

Once Michael had finished, Parker said, "I'm not going to give a diagnosis of a patient I haven't seen. But I think you might want to consider the possibility—just a possibility, mind you—that this is a case of dissociative fugue."

"A what?"

"It's a rare condition, but there have been cases of people who vanish from their homes and appear hundreds or thousands of miles away. They often show up with a new name and a new profession and no recollection of their former life."

"That sounds a lot like people faking amnesia," Michael said. "Nora wouldn't have done that. She loved her work." She loved *him*. Or so he had thought.

Parker said, "It's not something they do consciously. It's usually caused by some kind of trauma. Agatha Christie is supposed to have gone through this. She disappeared for several days and was found living under a different name. She didn't even recognize her husband when she met him. When she recovered, she had no memory of the intervening time."

"Still sounds like something fake."

"Maybe, maybe not. It's not as easy as it sounds to fake something like that, not consistently over a long period of time. According to her authorized biographer, Christie was still going to therapists twenty years later, trying to reconstruct her memories of the time she was missing. You'd think if she were faking it, she'd have come up with a better story."

Michael said doubtfully, "So you think that she is going to now come back to remembering her old life?" *Remembering me?*

"It's possible. I'm not about to commit myself without having seen the woman. Can you bring her up to Portland?"

"I can try. Parker, there's something about this situation that doesn't make any sense. I believed Nora when she said that she doesn't remember me. But if she's lost her identity, how did she acquire a new name? She's holding down a job, so she had to have help getting a social security card and a driver's license or some other kind of ID. And she's always surrounded by people." Catching her alone on the street had been a rare occurrence. "They don't like it when she talks to anyone outside her little circle. They might be honestly trying to protect her…but what if they're trying to *keep* her from recovering her memories? I've got to find a way to talk to her alone. If she's really suffering from amnesia, maybe I can help bring back her memories."

Parker said somberly, "I should warn you. Treating someone with this condition, if they have not regained their memories on their own, is often futile."

"If the real Nora is still there, deep down she'll want my help."

"Are you sure?" Parker said the words softly, but they sliced Michael with the precision of a scalpel. "People who suffer from this condition adopt a whole new identity. One theory is that it's so difficult to help them because these people have run away from themselves and don't want to come back. I do not think that anyone can help her if she does not want to be helped."

"I have to do something. I have to try."

Parker was silent a moment. Then he said, "Give me the name of her therapist. I'll ask around, see what I can find out."

"It's a Dr. Martha Green. I followed Nora to her place this afternoon."

"I'll let you know what I learn. And be careful. Don't fly off the handle."

But as Michael ended the call, he knew he was running out of time. This whole setup made no sense. What was Nora doing here? How had she ended up in a small town with no memory of him? It all made him uneasy.

Michael checked his phone to determine Nora's location. While she'd tended to the child who'd fallen, he'd taken the opportunity to slip her phone into his pocket and set it up to send out a signal. The blip of light showed that Nora was at her apartment. That middle-aged woman with the wild hair was always at Nora's side when she went out about the town.

Michael had to find a way to talk to Nora, tell her of her old life. He had to help her bring back her memories, and soon. Knowledge was the only thing that would protect her from whatever was going on in this town.

TWO

"It wasn't Tony's fault." Rachel felt as if she had explained this a hundred times, but Corrie still hadn't calmed down. "I... Well, it seemed harmless to walk home by myself."

Rachel put the mug of chamomile tea down on Corrie's kitchen table. For a woman who served coffee all day long, Corrie herself preferred herbal tea. Rachel never understood why; it always tasted like bitter weeds to her. But to avoid hurting Corrie's feelings, Rachel drank the tea all the same. This particular brew seemed stronger than usual. It was hard to choke down. Then again, right now her nerves were wound so tight it was hard to swallow at all. Perhaps it was the knowledge of what Rachel was planning to do next that turned her stomach.

"Rachel?" Corrie asked. "Is there something wrong with the tea?"

"Oh, no, not at all. It's lovely." Rachel pasted a bright smile on her face. "Honestly. And I hear what you're saying about being more careful. But… I mean, you have been so wonderful since my accident, but I need to try to do things on my own once in a while or I'll never get better."

Corrie sniffed, unimpressed by this reasoning. "You just rely on Dr. Green to tell you what treatment you need. You don't want a relapse or anything. Well, I'm going to go have a word with that sheriff." Corrie stood and turned to pick up her coat from the back of her chair.

Rachel took the opportunity to pour the rest of the cup into the sink before Corrie turned back. "Thank you for the tea. I really do feel better."

"Now, you go upstairs and have a nice rest, all right?" Corrie stood out in the alley and watched while Rachel climbed the outside stairs to her little attic apartment.

When she got to the landing outside the door, Rachel waved at Corrie and went inside, shutting the door behind her. Then swiftly, she went to the bedroom window over the porch. She craned her head until she saw Corrie's gray-brown head disappear around the corner toward the sheriff's office.

Rachel let out a sigh of relief. She slipped out down the stairs and headed down the alley in the opposite direction.

There was something she had to try, her own personal yardstick to measure her improvement. A quick trip, and she would be back before Corrie even noticed she'd been gone.

She was almost to the highway when she heard a car coming up behind her. A dark SUV, which slowed as it drew alongside her and then pulled over to the side of the road. The man in the trench coat got out. "We need to talk."

There were already more than enough people in her life who told her what to do. If she didn't stand up to this man, he was going to walk all over her, as well. "Was that a request? Sounded more like an order to me. Were you in the army or something?"

"Yes."

"Do women always salute and jump to obey your every command?"

"Evidently not," he said dryly. "My charm must be off today." He indicated the open door. "Let's sit in my car. I really do need to talk to you. Please."

The wind off the ocean was bitterly cold. Now that she had stopped moving, Rachel was acutely aware of its cutting edge. She wrapped her arms around herself, trying to keep warm. "You know, my mother warned me about getting into a car with a strange man. I want to trust you, but all my friends keep telling me to be more cautious. How do I know you're not some kind of serial killer?"

"You don't," the stranger said. He was not smiling. "You have no reason in the world to trust me. Trust your instinct. What does it tell you?"

"That you're dangerous," she said simply. "Or that you could be. All I know is that you've been acting strangely since the moment we met. You show up, make a few cryptic remarks and then walk off without a word of explanation. My friends all say I'm too trusting. Maybe they're right."

"I'm not the one who wants to harm you," he said softly. "And I really do need to talk with you. Please?"

A direct order she could push back on. But an appeal like that tugged on her heart, making her want to yield.

It made no sense to listen to this man. All the same, the warnings from Corrie and Dr.

Green and Tony didn't carry as much weight when she talked with him. Perhaps it was the way he looked at her when he said please. As if it mattered deeply, her trust. As if *she* mattered. Despite every rational reason she had to flee, her gut instinct was to stay. "All right." She climbed into the SUV.

Perhaps she was going crazy, after all. Still, it felt wonderful to be out of the wind. The soft leather seat was extremely comfortable, but she perched on the edge of it, ready to get out. Just in case.

He started the engine. "Can we go somewhere more private? I don't want anyone to see us."

"Easier to hide my body that way, too."

"I would *never* hurt you," he said, and the force of his sincerity struck her, powerful as the tide. Slowly, the car slid forward. "I don't want anyone to see us talking. Let's go to the lighthouse. It's more secluded, but you can walk away if you feel uncomfortable."

"That's outside the city limits! You can't take me there. Stop the car. Now."

Startled, he slowed the car. "Nora, I just want to talk. I won't strand you there."

"Let me out of here!" Her fingers scrabbled for the door handle.

The man reached over to grab her wrist. "Wait. You can't jump out of a moving car into traffic. And this road is too narrow to stop the car without getting hit. Let me find a safe spot to pull over."

"You're taking me out of town!" She was starting to hyperventilate, and her voice rose to a shriek. "I can't leave town! I can't! You have to stop the car!"

"Nora, please. Just let me get somewhere quiet—"

"Stop the car *now*!" She screamed the words at him. Rachel was sobbing, gasping for air. Something terrible was going to happen. She knew it. "You don't understand! I can't leave! I can't!"

"All right. It's all right." He turned down a side street into a more industrial area of mechanic shops and other businesses already closed for the day. He swerved around the corner of a garage and braked.

"I need to get out of this car." Even before the words escaped her mouth, she had wrenched the door open. She stood on the deserted side road, gulping in the chill air. Tears still poured down her face.

The stranger took a tissue out of the car's side door and handed it to her. "Please don't cry."

* * *

Nora accepted the tissue, but Michael doubted she even heard his words. He gave in to the impulse to put his arms around her, very gently, and put her head against his shoulder. She did not fight him. Indeed, he had the impression she was glad to have someone there. She leaned in, her whole body shaking with sobs. Michael had seen this woman go skydiving on a dare, grinning at him before jumping out of the plane. Now, she was panicking at the thought of driving down the street. It tore him up inside to think that he'd been the one to do this to her.

No. He'd only wanted to talk to her privately, to be safe. Someone else had done this to her—taken away her confidence, her belief in her own ability to stand up for herself.

That didn't make him feel any better about his own actions. In trying to save Nora, he had hurt her further. He'd failed her once, been out of town when she'd disappeared. He was not going to fail her again.

The sobs began easing off, her breathing growing more regular. She took a step back and his arms around her loosened. She wiped her eyes and focused on him. Gently, he said,

"You're better now? Nora, I am *so* sorry. I had no idea you would react like that."

Her breathing was still uneven. She shuddered as if trying to suppress a sob, but she said, calmly enough, "You could have asked me instead of trying to force me." He handed her another tissue and she wiped her eyes. "I don't even know your name."

It seemed the height of absurdity to introduce himself to her. But at least she was talking to him, even if she was still glaring. "My name is Michael Sullivan."

"And you're really a US marshal? I can't believe it."

He fished out his badge. "I have proof, if that helps."

"I should imagine that identification can be forged." She took the badge from him and examined it closely before returning it to him. "But if this is a fake, it's a good one."

Michael tucked his wallet back in his jacket. "I can provide references, but none of them live here." He hesitated. "The thought of leaving town makes you hysterical?"

She looked down, twisting the tissue between her hands. "I was in a car accident last year. That's why I had to have cosmetic surgery on my face. Ever since the accident, I can't face the thought of leaving town. It makes me sick to my stomach. I can't do it."

Her voice went lower, and he had to strain to catch her words. "Dr. Green says I'll get better in time. I have therapy sessions several times a week. Until I can get over this phobia, I have to stay here."

"I see." She was trapped in this town, imprisoned by fear.

The fog beaded her hair with moisture. It curled the strands, making her look younger, but she was shivering and he didn't think it was with fear this time. "Look, can we sit in the car? We won't go anywhere. I promise. I would never hurt you, Nora. Never."

She wiped away another stray tear. "I'm not sure why, but I'm inclined to believe you. Maybe it's because you're not very good at this kidnapping. Most kidnappers don't stop if you ask them to. All right. If it's all that important to you, I'll talk to you. So long as we stay within the city limits." She climbed back into the car and leaned over to close the door. "But you'll have to learn to start calling me by my name. Rachel."

Michael shut the door for her before going around to get in on his side. "I'll get the heater going."

She held her hands out over the heater vent as warmth filled the car. "That feels good." She looked at him. "When you grabbed me on the street—"

"You mean when I kept you from getting run over?"

She ignored this. "You expected me to know you." It was not a question.

Michael nodded. "We knew each other in the past."

"Somehow, I think I would remember you," she said wryly.

"There are reasons why you don't." He leaned forward. "I don't know how to say this, Nora, but—"

"My name is Rachel. I could show you my driver's license if that would help."

"Identification can be faked, or so I've been told."

"Then you'll just have to trust me," she shot back. "You've got me confused with someone else."

"I understand why you'd say that."

His calm resolve seemed to make her more alarmed rather than the reverse. Her voice rose. "Listen to me. My name is Rachel Garrett. I can tell you everything about myself. I was raised on a small farm near the Wallowa

Mountains. It was too far to get to a school, so my mother homeschooled me. When my parents died in a fire, I left. I had enough money from the sale of the farm that I didn't need to find work right away. I came here on vacation. Because of the car crash, I was stuck here in the hospital for a while. It's a nice place. I decided to stay. That's my story. Need more details? When I was young, my father used to take me trout fishing. Growing up, I had a cat named Pebbles. And—why are you looking at me like that?"

Michael hesitated. "I'm trying to think of how to tell you without upsetting you."

"Tell me what?"

He took a deep breath. "Everything you just said is a lie."

THREE

I might as well have told her I came from Mars. She was staring at Michael as if he'd lost all sense.

Michael had no idea how to convince her that he was telling the truth, but he had gone too far to stop now. He had this one chance to lay the facts out without anyone interrupting. He might not get another.

"I know this is hard for you to believe but it's true. You have been, I don't know, brainwashed somehow. I don't know how to bring you back to yourself. But I will try. Your name is Dr. Nora Stewart."

Her expression did not change. She sat there with a crease between her eyebrows as if *she* were worried about *him.* "My name," she said slowly, with deliberation, "is Rachel Garrett."

"I could show you photos, but I'm not sure if you'll see the resemblance. Your facial features have been altered by plastic surgery. I can tell you about yourself."

"That's very nice of you, but honestly—"

Michael went on regardless. "You work—worked—for a start-up company that specialized in cutting-edge medical research. You were developing some new drug that looked very promising." He spread his hands. "You didn't tell me all the details, but you sounded very excited about the possibilities."

It started to rain. Light drops ran down the windshield, blurring the view into a watercolor landscape of variations of gray. Beautiful, insubstantial, uncertain.

"Then your mood changed. You acted worried. I tried to get you to tell me what was going on, but you'd signed about a thousand different confidentiality agreements, and you couldn't tell me very much. You started spending long hours in the lab, missing dates—missing appointments," he corrected quickly. There was no telling how she would react if he told her about their relationship. It sounded exactly like the sort of thing a mad stalker would invent. He needed to establish some level of trust first.

"I went away on a job. I came back to find

you gone. Your apartment looked as if you had just stepped out."

She quirked one eyebrow, exactly the way Nora used to when something struck her as off. "You had a key to this woman's apartment?"

"Not exactly."

"How far from exactly?"

"Well, to be honest, I picked the lock. You really need to work on your security when you get back."

Her skeptical expression did not change. "And you didn't think to check at her work?"

"Of course, but all anyone would tell me at your work was that you had taken a leave of absence. I searched for you for months. I could not find any information on you. Finally, I tracked down a lead. I was going through crash reports when I came across an account of a woman who had gotten into a solo car accident the night that you disappeared. The name was wrong, but the car was the right make and model, plus the woman's age and height were a match, so I came to look for myself."

"To Sleepy Cove. To the Blue Whale Café."

"To you, Nora. I recognized you straight away."

"How? If my features have been altered, what makes you think I'm the same woman?"

Michael struggled to explain. "It's hard to put it into words, exactly. Your eyes haven't changed. I recognized them immediately. But it's more than that. It's your body language, the way you tilt your head when you're considering a question, the lift of your eyebrow when I say something that doesn't make sense to you. I'm not making this up. It really is you."

"I see."

"Going by the look on your face, I'd say you don't believe a word I'm saying."

"Well, no," she said frankly. "But I was trying to be tactful. I can see *you* believe it."

"After I left you this afternoon, I talked to a friend of mine. A… Well, he's a doctor. I think he could help you. He had some interesting things to say about your condition."

"That's a coincidence. I was just thinking that I could take you to see Dr. Green. She is very kind, and I think perhaps she could help *you.*"

"I am not delusional," Michael said stiffly.

She went on, in that patient manner, "If you look at this logically, you will see how absurd your whole premise is. Yes, I've had issues with anxiety since the car accident. I get nervous, jump at shadows. But that doesn't mean I've forgotten who I am or where I come from."

Michael leaned back against his seat in disgust. "You've completely bought in to this false identity."

"And how exactly do you think I ended up with, as you call it, a false identity?"

She was still humoring him. He couldn't tell her all of his suspicions about an active conspiracy against her. Not until he had some kind of proof to offer. Instead, he temporized. "I'm not sure. Not yet. But I've been thinking. Do you remember any details about the car accident that landed you here? Pretty convenient that it caused you to have cosmetic surgery."

She shook her head, but she shifted in the seat and would not meet his eyes. Ah, that made her uneasy.

He probed, "Not even driving in the car before the accident?"

She turned away, her shoulders hunched, seeming to take a great deal of interest in the raindrops running down the windshield. "It's quite normal to not remember a car accident."

"So you can't even be sure you were driving the car when it was wrecked. All you know for a fact is that you woke up in a hospital covered in bandages. And another thing—don't you think it's odd that you have people following you every time you step outside your door?"

"You mean people like Tony or Corrie? They want to be sure I don't have an anxiety attack. They're my friends."

"Or jailers."

"Stop." She actually put her hands over her ears. "I am not going to listen to this. I trust Corrie and Tony—and—and everybody in this town."

Gently, Michael pulled her hands away and held them between his own. He rubbed her fingers. They were chilled, but Nora didn't seem to notice. "All right. We won't talk about your guard dogs. Look at the facts. A fire that takes away your parents and any mementos of your past. A car crash that isolates you in a small town. Cosmetic surgery, which alters your appearance. All ties to your past have been severed."

"Except for my memories."

"Memories are more fragile than people think. Any alcoholic who's ever gone on a bender can tell you that a sufficient quantity of alcohol can wipe out short-term memory. You told me once that your boss wanted to explore the possibility of developing pharmaceuticals that could induce a long-term state of amnesia. You couldn't give me any specific details, but apparently the idea was that the drugs would be used to help traumatized patients who needed the chance to step back from painful memories, give them time to heal. And Parker—my doctor friend—said what you have is a type of retrograde amnesia called a dissociative fugue."

She opened her mouth as if to object, but Michael forged on. "Well, what's there to stop someone from using medications like these on an unwilling subject? It would fit in this case. Are they giving you drugs?"

"Yes," she said reluctantly. "To help with the anxiety issues I've had since the car crash. And I have therapy sessions, as well."

"Does your therapy include hypnosis?"

"Yes."

"So you could have been given drugs to take away your old identity. And then hypnosis sessions would plant new memories, false ones." Michael struggled to control the rage inside him.

She started to shake her head, and he put up his hand. "Wait. Before you tell me I'm crazy, consider this. How did you know what to do this afternoon when the little girl might have been injured?"

"It was basic first aid."

"It was the kind of thing Nora would have done."

She looked down at her hands. Her voice was low. "I just knew what to do without thinking. As if a stranger were operating my body. How can I know something and not know that I know it?" She looked up, and for the first time he saw doubt in her eyes. "Tell me about this Nora woman."

Was he actually getting through to her? "What do you want to know?"

"Everything."

Michael answered the questions as best he could. Nora's Ivy League education, earning advanced degrees before coming out to Oregon to work for a biomedical firm. Meeting Michael in church.

He would have been heartened by her curiosity—if her dark eyes had not been so filled with fear. He could not begin to imagine how she must feel. It must be like having a stranger living in the back of your mind or as if you were a stranger to yourself.

She heard him out silently, with just a pinch of a frown between her eyebrows. When he finished, she said quietly, "Then how do you explain my ending up here?"

Michael said cautiously, "I think someone

might have arranged for you to be brought here."

"Do you have any idea how crazy that sounds?"

"I don't have all the answers yet. I'm still trying to fit all the pieces of the puzzle together. But yes, I believe that's the truth." Michael had an idea of who could be behind it, but he didn't think she was ready to hear any more details just yet. She was having a hard enough time believing him already.

She let her breath out in a little huff. Amazing how much skepticism could be conveyed in a single puff of air. "You call it truth. I call it fantasy. An awful lot of coincidences would have to have occurred for your story to be true. Do you seriously expect me to believe that the whole town is in on this charade?"

"They don't need to be. One or two people in key positions could keep an eye on you, manage you. The rest of the townsfolk could be ordinary people getting on with their daily lives. That's why I need to get you out of here. There's no way to tell who you can trust."

"I'm sorry." She held up a hand to stop him. "I don't mean to hurt your feelings, but this doesn't make any sense. Your whole tale is impossible."

"Nora—"

"Stop calling me that!"

Michael hated the idea of calling her Rachel. It would be like admitting Nora wasn't coming back to him. But maybe he should try, at least for now, to think of her as Rachel. She wasn't ready to accept her real identity, not yet. Nora always had been too stubbornly independent for her own good.

Nora—no, Rachel—frowned at him, folding her arms. "Why would anyone go through all that trouble? Why would anyone want to control me? I'm just a waitress."

"I think that your disappearance is connected to your work." Michael leaned forward. Her identifying herself as Rachel was a protective suit of armor. She didn't realize it was also a prison. He would never break her free until he could find a way to persuade her. "Because you—because Dr. Nora Stewart was brilliant at her work. You had a vast reserve of knowledge in a highly lucrative field. In that case, they would not want to lose you as a resource."

Rachel tilted her head to one side, considering this. For a moment, Michael almost dared to hope. Then she patted his hand. "Seriously, I do think you would feel better if you talked to Dr. Green."

"You could always go get a second opinion about your treatment," Michael said, desperate now. "That is something any qualified doctor would agree to. I have a friend in Portland who would meet with you. It won't hurt to talk to him. I would trust him with my life. I would trust him with yours."

"In Portland. Do you see a problem with that?"

"You could be sedated for the trip?"

"No," Rachel said with decision. "I will stay where I am. I know who I am and I know the people here. And if I get better—no, *when*—it will be on my own terms."

Michael wondered if she could hear the note of fear in her voice. She was clinging so desperately to her current identity. "But what if the people you are trusting to help you aren't really looking out for your best interest?"

"I won't listen to this." Rachel pressed her lips together until her mouth flattened into a thin line. "These are my friends. I know that they only want what is best for me." She put her hand on the door handle. "Well. All this was very interesting. But I can see it's stopped raining, so this is a good time to go."

"You still don't believe a word I've said." For a moment there, he'd thought that his words had reached her. But she was barricaded too securely against any change to her prison.

"Do you want me to give you an honest answer or a polite truth?"

"Honesty," Michael said. "Always."

She twisted around to face him. "Then in all honesty, I think you're so obsessed with finding this Nora woman that you're trying to persuade yourself there's something wrong when there isn't. The thought of an evil mastermind running a conspiracy in Sleepy Cove is beyond absurd. Everything is just the way it looks. This is a nice town. People are pleasant here. If you stay a few days, get to know people, you'll see."

"Oh, I'll stay," he said grimly. "This whole setup smells wrong. I can't leave until I know you'll be safe."

"No one is going to hurt me here." She opened the car door. "And I'm not alone."

"Wait." Michael took an old envelope out of his pocket and scribbled on it. "Here. This is my friend—the doctor's—phone number. And here is mine. Call Parker if you want to talk about the medication you've been prescribed, or anything else about the treatment that you would like a second opinion on. And call me if you ever feel threatened. Or text me. It's better if we're not seen together until you leave." He reached out to hand her the envelope.

Rachel accepted the paper with obvious reluctance, but she did put it in her pocket. "Thanks. I guess. I imagine you're trying to help me. I just think you've confused me with someone else."

Michael said carefully, "I realize it's a lot to ask of you to trust me."

Rachel looked at him, and the tense line of her mouth relaxed, a barely perceptible softening. "Look at it from my point of view. You are a total stranger who comes up to me and tells me I need to rearrange my entire life. That everything I have ever believed in isn't real. If someone came up to you with that tale, how would you react?"

Michael had failed. Without proof, she would never take the danger she was in seriously.

Rachel trudged back to her apartment with her hands in her pockets, her head down against the wind that blew her hair out of its ponytail.

Life just wasn't fair. The only truly attractive man in Sleepy Cove turned out to be not only delusional but obsessed with some other woman. Michael was so fixated on this Nora that he couldn't even see Rachel standing right before him. Nothing poisoned the self-esteem like being called some other woman's name. And why did he have to have a deep persuasive voice that made her want to agree with him, even if he was talking complete nonsense?

Michael kept his word, at least. He stopped standing out in front of the café. She saw him at odd moments—on the corner of the street on her way to work, outside the storage room on her break.

He never made eye contact, never spoke to her directly. Which is not to say he did not communicate.

The following afternoon, just as the lunch-time rush was petering out, Rachel's phone made the beep that indicated a text.

If I can bring Parker here, will you see him?

Rachel shifted so that her back was to the customers. Stealthily, her thumbs flew over the keys.

If Dr. Green does not mind. How did you get my phone number?

Another beep. Rachel muted the phone before reading Michael's message.

Don't speak to her about this. She might be involved with the people who want to keep you here. In fact, she is probably the ringleader.

That is absurd. She has gone out of her way to help me. I can't believe this. You're trying to turn me against everyone I trust. Plus, you didn't answer my question about how you got my phone number.

The discussion made Rachel feel grimy, tarnished by disloyalty for questioning a woman who had shown her nothing but kindness. Dr. Green was the only doctor Rachel could really trust.

My friend Parker says he's heard some shifty rumors about your Dr. G. She used to work at a mental institution near Salem, but she left last year abruptly. Apparently, she had a reputation for being too aggressive toward the patients. And here's another thing. She just arrived in Sleepy Cove and set up her clinic shortly before you arrived.

Rachel threw a quick glance over her shoulder before replying.

Pure coincidence. I will not condemn my friends. Enough already. I trust Dr. G. She only wants what is best for me. Don't text me anymore.

Rachel hit Send. Before she could reconsider, she deleted Michael's contact information from her phone and turned it off.

"What are you doing with your phone?" Mrs. Gibbs, the dentist's wife, was looking at her curiously.

Rachel put her phone in her pocket. "I was just checking the weather report." Turning away, she busied herself clearing the last of the lunch plates. The last thing she needed was for people to think that she was starting to believe in conspiracy theories.

She could still feel the other woman's eyes on her. Time for a distraction. "Mrs. Gibbs, tell me something. Don't you think it's odd that I never hear from old friends?"

"What do you mean?"

"Well… Corrie goes to see her friends in Eugene nearly every week. Dr. Green has colleagues from Salem that she meets up with. Even Tony gets together with his old police buddies in Portland for the occasional barbecue. Yet I never leave and no one ever comes to visit me. Don't you think that's odd?"

"Well, of course you don't leave. I wouldn't either, not if I'd had that horrific accident myself."

"But why don't I have any friends come visit from outside of this town? It's as if I don't exist to the outside world." Her isolated upbringing on the farm had meant few opportunities to forge friendships, but surely she must have made some. Why couldn't she now recall a single one?

"My, you're full of questions today." Mrs. Gibbs laughed as if Rachel had been making a joke.

Miss Trant chimed in, "You go right ahead and ask questions, Rachel. You've earned it. I heard about that business with the child the other day. The girl's mother has been going around town telling everyone how wonderful you were."

"What child?" Corrie looked bewildered.

"Oh, that." Rachel explained about the near accident.

Corrie listened, frowning. "And you took it on yourself to help the girl? Why didn't you call 911?"

Rachel stopped to consider. "I don't know

why I didn't call. I—well, I guess I just acted on instinct."

"So that's why you were standing out on the highway. I'd been wondering about that." Corrie flipped the sign on the door to Closed. "Well, ladies, if you don't mind, it's been a long day. I want to go home and make Rachel some chamomile tea." She patted Rachel on the shoulder.

Rachel couldn't help looking over her shoulder as she and Corrie walked home. The shadows were empty.

Well, of course no one was lurking there. Rachel squashed down the irrational feeling of disappointment. She should be glad that there was no sign of Michael Sullivan. Everything was back to normal. There was no conspiracy against her. Nothing was wrong.

That night, Rachel dreamed. She often did, but once she woke up, she could never remember anything specific.

This dream was different. It felt more alive, each detail sharp and precise. She was in a boat, being rowed across a lake. The water was an incredibly vivid blue. Sunlight sparkled on the surface like scattered diamonds.

Rachel narrowed her eyes, squinting against

the sunlight to look up at the man opposite, who was rowing the boat. It was the strange man, Michael Sullivan. Except now he was casually dressed and he was laughing down at her. The happiness on his face made him look years younger, as if a burden had been lifted from him.

Rachel felt free, as well, her whole body filled with joy. Michael's lips moved, but she could not make out what he was saying, though she strained to hear him.

He leaned forward and just for a brief second he brushed his lips against hers in a kiss so intensely sweet that she woke up, opening her eyes into the cold and the dark of her little attic apartment. She lay there, her whole body filled with a desire to escape back into the dream. Where she had felt warm and comforted and safe.

Through the gap between the curtain and the window, she could see dawn just breaking. Rachel got dressed quickly, trying not to think about the dream. About the sensation of his lips meeting hers.

She slipped down the steps that led from her attic apartment to the alley. Carefully, she made her way through the back streets to the edge of town. The sun was just rising over the hills, throwing sharp-edged shadows across the pavement. The town was wrapped in the hushed stillness of early morning. A few houses showed lights in the windows, but no one was out on the street yet. Perfect. She could get there and back before anyone knew she'd been gone.

The city boundary lay maybe a hundred yards past the last building. It was marked by a sign that proclaimed You're Leaving Sleepy Cove! Come Back Soon!

As usual, the sight of that cheerful sign made Rachel break into a sweat. Every instinct screamed at her to stop, to turn around. Her steps got slower and slower, and she had to fight to keep moving. Nausea roiled in her stomach. One step, then another, as if fighting her way through the surf with the tide flowing against her. *I can do this.*

This was her test. Her private ritual to see if she was getting better. The day she managed to walk out past the city limits would be the day she knew she was on the road to recovery.

Even walking slowly, she finally made it to the signpost. All it would take was one step forward, and she'd have broken through the barrier in her mind.

Rachel put her hand on the smooth metal of

the supporting pole and looked ahead. A lonely road, disappearing around the curve. At the thought of going any farther, her legs began to shake as if they were made of jelly. Rachel leaned against the pole and took in a breath that was half-sob. She couldn't do it. Not today.

"Next week," she whispered. "I'll try again then." She trudged back into town, head down and hands in her pockets. Paper crinkled under her fingers. She drew out the envelope with the phone numbers. Maybe Michael was right. Another doctor might have suggestions on ways she could get over this phobia. She might try calling him.

She shoved the envelope back in her pocket, crumpling the paper. Maybe it was a bad idea to call a friend of Michael's. She'd find a different doctor. If she searched online, she could check out their credentials and see if she liked the sound of them.

The wind was at her back now, whipping her hair out of its ponytail and blowing strands across her face. She didn't see the white van until it screeched to a stop by the side of the road. A man jumped out and shoved a cloth against her face. Rachel barely had time to register the smell of some sharp, acrid chemical before she lost consciousness.

FOUR

Before dawn, Michael had driven back to the cabin. He wasn't happy about leaving Nora—Rachel—alone, even for a few hours, but if he pushed her too much, she might turn against him.

He was not going to make that mistake again.

That had always been the problem between them. His first instinct was still to just solve the problem and be done with it. Nora always wanted to *talk*, discuss her feelings and his, find a solution that would work for everyone.

In the past, he had grown impatient, tried to move on and deal with a problem before Nora was ready. Not anymore.

The final time they'd fought, it had been about her boss, Dr. Vance. Something about Vance had always struck Michael as shady. He couldn't put a finger on what the problem was exactly, until the night that Vance had taken credit for Nora's work at an awards dinner. Michael had been furious. He'd urged Nora to call out Dr. Vance in public. Nora had refused. She'd handle it in her own way, she'd said.

That had been the last time he'd seen her before her disappearance. When he'd come back and noticed her gone, Michael had wondered if their argument that night had been the trigger that caused her to leave. Even now, when he was convinced someone had kidnapped her, he could not shake the feeling that he'd been in the wrong to push her.

Regardless of what or who had caused Nora to disappear, Michael had learned his lesson. He was going to do whatever it took to earn her trust. Get her to listen to him.

He'd rented an old hunter's cabin high in the Coast Range hills and stocked it with food and bottled water. Primitive living at best, the place was off-the-grid and cell phone reception was nonexistent. If Rachel continued to cling to the notion that she had to stay within the city limits, Michael would probably have to find somewhere closer to hole up. But for now, this place was cheap and met his needs. His resources were not infinite. He'd taken leave from his job and spent a couple months tracking Rachel down. However long it took, he was going to see that she got the help she needed.

The sun was above the hills by the time he had showered and changed his clothes. He rubbed his jaw. He should shave, but he felt uneasy being out of touch with Rachel for any longer than absolutely necessary. There was a small town a few miles away, where the highway crossed a river. It was the only place around where Michael could get a clear signal on his phone.

He needed to check on Rachel. He used to call her every night, even when he was out of town, just to hear the smile in her voice when she said, "I was hoping you were going to call." Warmth had swept through him every time. The last few months had been torture, not knowing where she was or even if she were still alive.

Now, he'd found her. And at the same time, he'd lost her. She had no recollection of their time together, of all the joy they'd shared.

No memory of the night he'd slipped the engagement ring on her finger.

The ring was gone now, of course. He hadn't seen it on her finger. It must have been swept away along with every other memento of her former life. Including him.

Michael pulled over on the edge of the small town, down by the river, and took out his phone. Before he could call Rachel, his phone rang beneath his hand.

"Sullivan?" When he answered the call, his boss's gravelly voice sounded in his ear. "Have you finally come to your senses? Ready to come back to work?"

"Lynch. Good morning. I need more time. It's going to take a little longer to sort things out."

"I understand you want to track down your girlfriend, but I can't keep your job open forever. You expected to go on leave for a week or two. Not months. I can't put you on indefinite leave, even without pay. We need to get someone in to take up the work if you can't— or won't—come back."

"Just a little more time," Michael said. "A couple weeks."

"Well…" his boss hesitated.

"I wouldn't ask if it weren't important." Michael had served under Lynch in the army. When you served together in a combat zone, you developed a bond that was hard to break.

Lynch sighed. "All right. I'm going to be out of the office on vacation, hiking up in Canada for a week. I won't be able to deal with administrative issues until I get back."

"Thank you. I really appreciate it." On impulse, Michael added, "Before you go—I need some information. It might be related to Nora's disappearance. Can you look into the background of a Dr. Christopher Vance? He's the CEO of a biomedical company outside of Eugene."

"What do you want to know?"

"Anything, really. Who is behind his funding? Does he have controlling shares in the company? I'd look it up myself, but here on the coast internet access is not that reliable."

"I'll let you know what I can find out. But you haven't got much time left to do any digging. Once I come back, I'll have to start putting through the paperwork for letting you go." Lynch sighed, the weariness in his tone clear even over the phone. "I remember when this job was all you wanted to do. If that's changed, maybe you need to rethink your priorities."

"I will. Thank you, sir." Michael ended the call.

Rachel hadn't answered his text. Was she avoiding him? After a few minutes, he tried again. No response.

Maybe she had blocked him altogether. Michael checked the app that showed the location of Rachel's phone overlaid with a map.

The signal came through clearly, but Rachel wasn't at her home or the café. She wasn't even in town. The little flashing light showed that she was up in the hills and on the move.

Michael's fingers clenched around the slim phone as though he could choke answers from it. There was no way she would have left town of her own volition. Michael started the car, tires screeching as he peeled away from the curb. The signal was well into the hills, not too far from where he was. The cell reception would give out soon. If he didn't catch up with her fast, he'd lose her. Again.

Rachel woke with her cheek pressed against cold metal that vibrated in a steady rhythm. She was lying on her side, with her hands and legs tied with some kind of cord. It bit into her wrists when she tried to flex them.

A van. Vague memories stirred in the back of her mind. A white van. A man grabbing her.

In the front, papers rustled. A voice, a man's light tenor. "Man, do you have to keep it so messy in here? I can't put my feet anywhere without stepping on fast-food wrappers."

"Hey, where would you be without me and

my van? You'd never have been able to pull off this job."

"All I'm saying is I don't know how you can find anything in here," the man grumbled.

"Relax, Pete. What are you looking so worried for? Nobody saw us grab the woman."

"I was just wondering… Why do they want her so bad?"

Craning her neck, Rachel could just see the two men in the front seats. Rain splattered the windshield. Clouds darkened the sky. Beyond that, nothing else but steep wooded hills.

It was growing dark, though the clock on the dashboard showed only midafternoon. The windshield wipers swept away white flecks mingled with the raindrops now. Snow. The dark clouds promised more. She shivered.

"Who cares? We're getting paid good money." The driver's voice was deeper, with that guttural rasp that came from heavy smoking. "Nobody saw us. She doesn't start work at that café for a couple more hours. By that time, we'll already have dropped her off and picked up the money. Then I'm heading straight to the poker tables."

"You're not getting any more money from me." Pete sounded resentful. "I brought you in on this deal. I paid my debt. And I'm not taking on a job like this anymore. I don't like it."

The other man laughed. Not a pleasant sound. The van began to wind up a steep hill, swerving around hairpin curves. The engine whined as the van climbed higher. Rachel was helpless to stop her body from sliding back and forth across the floor. They had trussed her up without bothering to secure her to anything.

Rachel tried to make sense of the situation. Her thinking was still slowed from the drug. But there was something else, a realization that loomed larger and larger until she had to face it.

I've left Sleepy Cove.

The thought hit Rachel like a sneaker wave, coming up out of nowhere and threatening to drown her in panic. She fought to control the urge to vomit. A cloth gag bit into the sides of her mouth so tightly that a soft moan escaped her.

The driver shifted and glanced over his shoulder. "She's waking up. You didn't give her enough of that stuff."

"Hey!" Pete was indignant. "I used the dosage he gave me. He said if I gave her too much, she'd get sick. You want to clean that up?"

Rachel paid no attention to their bickering.

Terror seized her, a tsunami that built higher and higher, rising until it toppled over onto her. Her breath came in shallow gasps. She could not control it. She was trembling. Desperately, she thrashed from side to side, frantic to escape. The bonds on her wrists and ankles dug into her skin, but she was past caring. She heard their conversation, but the words held little meaning.

"What's going on with her? Look at her, Jake! She's really freaking out."

"She can't go anywhere. Let her have her fun."

"I'm serious, man. She's going to choke or something. I don't think she can breathe. Pull over."

The van swerved to one side and slowed abruptly. Rachel slid across the floor, landing up against the wall of the van. She bent over, gasping for oxygen. Her vision dimmed.

A chilly gust of air blasted her as the back doors were flung open. Cold hands pawed her. Her gag was loosened. She gulped in air. She was shivering violently now, unable to control herself.

"Hey, lady, calm down, okay? Seriously, Jake, she's cut herself." The bonds around her wrists were loosened. "They don't want her to show up bleeding all over the place." Pete chafed her hands. His tousled blond hair hung over his eyes, but Rachel could see that he was a young man, almost a boy. "There. That better, lady?"

Rachel could not answer. She was getting her breathing under control, but she didn't trust herself to form coherent sentences. She nodded.

"Hurry up," Jake growled. He was a bigger man, with thick dark eyebrows and a beer belly. "We gotta get on the road. Somebody sees us by the side of the road, they'll stop and ask questions."

"Who's going to see us? We're halfway up a mountain. And it's starting to snow."

"Great. Just what we needed. Hurry it up."

"I'm going to retie her bonds, not so tight this time." Pete sliced the zip tie around her ankles and chafed them. His hands were rough and freezing, but she could feel the blood flow returning.

"Th-th-thank you," she choked out.

Pete avoided her gaze. A considerate kidnapper? Somehow, Rachel doubted it. But he didn't want her dead. Not yet, anyway. That gave her a tiny amount of leverage. She had to act subdued and wait for her moment. Lull him into thinking her harmless, then seize any opportunity to get free and escape.

Her body shook with great wracking spasms, but they were easing up. She could think more clearly now.

Lord, I know You are with me, even here. Help me to be strong and face whatever comes.

She didn't have much time. Once they tied her back up and closed her in the van again, she'd be helpless. Her panic attack had given her a brief window of opportunity. Rachel tensed her muscles.

"Hurry up. It's freezing out here." Jake shoved his hands into his pockets. Rachel noticed the bulge in the right-hand pocket. A gun?

"I left the zip ties in the front." Pete stood up. "Watch her."

"Yeah, right. Where's she going to go?" Nevertheless, Jake moved his right hand in his pocket. It *was* a gun. Rachel was sure of it.

Jake reached inside his jacket with his other hand and pulled out a cell phone. He tapped some buttons, keeping an eye on Rachel.

Rachel hunched her shoulders and kept her gaze on the ground, projecting defeat. Her muscles tensed.

A muffled call from the front of the van.

"Where do you keep the zip ties? I can't find anything in this heap."

"In the glove compartment." Jake took another step away, angling his phone to try for better reception.

This was the best chance she was going to get. Rachel sprang up. In an instant, she was off the road, sliding down the steep hillside and into the woods. She heard the men shouting behind her, but she did not look back.

Pine branches whipped across her face, stinging her. The woods were dark, shadowed with early twilight. Her feet sunk into the loose soil, mud mixed with slush. The going was no easier for her pursuers. Guttural curses from Jake and heavy panting. They were getting closer.

Light gleamed ahead of her, outlining the trees. She was coming to a clearing. Nowhere to hide.

Rachel plunged out of the trees and discovered herself on the side of a slope so steep it was almost a cliff. She stopped suddenly, throwing out her hands in an attempt to catch her balance. Her feet slid out from under her and she was falling, tumbling, rolling down the hillside.

She came to an abrupt stop, caught by an

outcropping of rock that broke her fall. It felt as if it had broken her ribs, as well, but she was able to get to her feet again, panting. She had slid down a few hundred feet to a lower loop of the road they'd been climbing.

Above her, the men cursed. There was no way for them to follow the path she'd inadvertently taken. They were climbing back up to the van. The sight galvanized her. Every moment of freedom meant a chance to escape somehow.

Without further thought, she ran across the road and into the trees below. The road had looped around several hairpin turns. If she could avoid cliffs, she could possibly hide in the woods. Not much chance for survival in the mountains at night in winter, but she might be able to find a cabin. In the still mountain air, she could clearly hear the doors of the van slam shut and the engine roar to life. The sound of another car, as well, coming up the road toward them.

She slid down onto a lower section of the road and ran full-out. That *was* another car she could hear, driving fast. The van was coming down the hill now, brakes screeching as it slowed for a hairpin turn. Could she make contact with the new car before the van caught up with her?

A dark SUV came around the curve toward her. Her heart leaped. She recognized the car even before Michael Sullivan braked to a stop by her. He rolled down the window. "Get in, Nora!"

For once, Rachel didn't stop to correct him. She was out of breath, anyway. She ducked around to the passenger side and jumped in. The van came into sight, heading straight toward them.

Michael reversed quickly, and the SUV spun around. As he put the car in Drive, a shot rang out. Something clipped the side of the window and Michael sagged sideways.

She braced him. "Are you hit?"

Michael spoke between gritted teeth. "Stay back." He pulled his gun out from under his coat and aimed carefully, fired once. In the side mirror, Rachel saw the van lurch to one side, its front near tire flattened. The van skidded off the road and landed up against a tree.

Michael floored it.

She glanced over and saw a streak of red trailing down his forehead.

"You're hurt!"

"A graze," Michael muttered. "Not as bad as it looks."

"That's good, because it looks dreadful."

"Hang on." Michael was speeding down the road before she had her seat belt on.

She glanced at him. "I need to check out that wound. You're losing a lot of blood."

"Once I put some distance between us and that fool with his bad aim. If the snow keeps falling, he'll be able to track us once he fixes the tire I shot out. I want to get to a lower elevation. He can't track us through rain."

Sure enough, the snow was turning to rain against the windshield wipers. Michael took a turn off the highway onto a side road. He seemed to know where he was going, so she asked no questions. There was no sign of a van pursuing them. Rachel began to breathe more freely, though she could not stop shivering. Michael glanced at her and turned up the car's heater so that blessed warmth flowed over her.

After a few minutes, they turned off onto a dirt track that began to climb uphill again. The trees on either side nearly touched overhead. The light was dimmer here. The road climbed steadily upward. A few snowflakes spiraled out of the storm clouds, but the road was sheltered from the full force of the storm.

Michael wiped his hand across his forehead. When he lowered his arm, his sleeve was wet with blood, red and glistening. Rachel said, "You need to pull over and let me drive. You're in no shape to be behind the wheel. I need to take you to the hospital in Sleepy Cove."

"You'd be signing my death warrant." Michael swerved onto a dirt track so narrow the tree branches scraped the sides of the SUV. Then the track broadened into a circle wide enough to turn around.

Braking to a stop, he turned off the engine. A sigh escaped him, as if he'd laid down a burden. Then Michael leaned forward until he was slumped over the steering wheel. His eyes closed, and his face turned the color of sour milk. He looked dead.

FIVE

Please, Lord. Please don't let him be dead.

Frantically, Rachel shook Michael's shoulder. He murmured but did not move. The blood was still flowing freely down his head. It splashed across her fingers, warm and viscous. Her breath caught on a sob. "Can you hear me?"

Michael groaned something that sounded like "Yes." He straightened, fingers clenched around the steering wheel for support.

Rachel looked around in all directions. Apart from a tiny shed filled with firewood, there was nothing but a solid wall of trees. "Where do we go from here?"

"The cabin is just up the trail." Michael fumbled for the door handle.

Rachel hopped out of the car. Her feet sank into fresh snow that came up above her shoes. The cold stung against her skin. When she helped Michael out of the car, he leaned on her heavily. Rachel suppressed a wince. During her flight down the hillside, she'd been too caught up in the moment to notice how many bruises she'd acquired, but now her body was busy making a tally, and it was a long list. It felt as if every part of her had had a close encounter with a rock along the way.

Rachel gritted her teeth and put her arm around his waist, struggling to keep her footing under his added weight. There was a narrow gap in the trees that she supposed might conceivably be called a trail, but no sign of a cabin.

The snow began to fall in earnest as Rachel helped Michael up through the trees. The cold soaked through the thin canvas of her running shoes. She hadn't dressed for a hike this morning; she only wore a thin cotton sweater and jeans. Once they got soaked, hypothermia was going to be a serious possibility.

Michael's trench coat offered some protection from the elements, but it was a garment designed for city wear. It snagged on low branches and caught on any deadfall on the ground. Michael was sweating now, his face ghastly white. He pressed his mouth into a thin line and kept his eyes fixed on the track ahead.

Rachel pressed closer to Michael, shivering now with great wracking spasms. They couldn't go on like this much farther.

Coming around a turn, she spotted a wood-shingled roof through the trees. The small cabin blended in with the woods so well it was hard to see, especially in the fast-growing dusk.

They staggered up the porch steps together. Rachel grasped the ice-cold metal of the door-knob and twisted. To her surprise and relief, it wasn't locked. The door opened into the half-darkness of a cold, clammy room. Rachel supported Michael across the room and onto an old sagging couch.

Rachel straightened. The place was deserted, but there was a woodstove in the corner and split logs piled nearby. "I'll start a fire before we do anything else. I'm sure whoever owns this place would understand."

Michael murmured something that might have been agreement. He lay back against the faded cushions and closed his eyes. Blood still trickled down from his temple.

Thankfully, a fire had been already laid in the stove, with matches ready on the side table by the couch. The fire caught quickly, eager yellow tongues of flame licking the kindling into life-giving warmth.

An oil lamp stood on a table. Once lit, it provided a homey glow to the plain pine walls. In a little nook off the main room, she located pots and pans. Bottled water was stored in a cupboard. She poured water into a pan and put it on the woodstove to heat.

Michael hadn't moved, but his breathing sounded more regular. It was the first time she had taken the opportunity to look closely at him when he was not aware of her scrutiny.

He slept with the exhaustion of a man who had been pushing himself for too long with too little rest. She noticed dark circles under his eyes. "You poor man," she murmured. "How long have you been searching for your Nora?" Rachel couldn't repress a twinge of envy toward the woman who had been the focus of such devotion.

Rachel set the lamp next to the couch and bent close to examine the wound on Michael's head. Sliding her hands through his hair, she felt the familiar warm stickiness of blood. He twitched as her fingers explored his scalp, but he didn't wake up.

Encouraged, she methodically checked over the rest of his body. No other wounds. Good.

His trench coat had protected most of his clothing from the cold. She removed his boots and rolled up his trousers so nothing damp lay against his skin. It would take a while for the heat from the stove to warm him. Well, if the owner stocked the cabin with firewood, maybe he had blankets and something Rachel could use for a bandage.

The rest of the cabin was simply furnished. A short hallway led to a small bedroom containing a bed covered in a quilt. A chest by the couch held thick woolen blankets, smelling faintly of cedar. A door on one side revealed a very basic bathroom with a simple first aid kit, including bandages and antiseptic swabs.

Rachel covered Michael up with one of the blankets. Heat was radiating through the room now, taking the edge off its clammy, stale feeling. Her clothes were still unpleasantly damp, and she moved closer to the fire, warming herself.

Once the water began to boil, Rachel took it off the stove and started to clean Michael's wound. Her touch seemed to rouse him. He peered at her between narrowed eyes and muttered, "Dry clothes…in suitcase."

"Later," Rachel soothed. "I need to tend to this wound first."

"For you," Michael muttered. His eyes closed again and he lay still.

Rachel applied antiseptic and bandaged the wound. Then she sat back, looking him over. He didn't look so pale now, and he was resting comfortably. In sleep, the worry lines on his face relaxed—he looked younger, vulnerable. A day's growth of stubble shadowed his jaw. Maybe this cabin had a razor somewhere.

In the bedroom closet, she found a man's jeans and a flannel shirt in about Michael's size. Evidently, this must be where Michael had been staying. A suitcase sat on the floor next to the bed. Rachel heaved it up onto the bed and opened it. But instead of a razor, she found more men's clothing. That must be what he had meant. He had noticed her shivering.

Rachel replaced her wet clothing with an oversize sweatshirt lined with fleece and some sweatpants that she had to roll up several times. By the time she padded back into the main room in wool socks, her feet finally warm, her spirits had risen. It was a marvelous feeling to sit in the armchair by the fire, snug and dry, while outside the wind blew a wild wailing and the snow piled upon the windowsill.

She'd been riding an emotional roller coaster

for hours. She was wrung out, emotionally. And somehow, the experience, horrifying as it had been, felt cathartic. Finally letting herself accept the fear instead of barricading herself against it had purged a burden from her.

In the back of her mind, a relentless thought nagged at her. *I have to get back to Sleepy Cove. I have to get back...* But there was another part of her that was content to sit, watching Michael sleep. Rachel wanted to reach out and smooth the mussed-up hair from his forehead. She felt fiercely protective of him.

The strength of this feeling surprised her. It seemed to come out of nowhere, surfacing unexpectedly as if from the depths of a lake.

A window by the stove looked out on the path they had taken to come here. The snow was falling thickly now, covering up the evidence of their footprints, hiding their trail away from any possible pursuit. They were in a safe haven. For the moment.

Michael woke suddenly from a deep sleep, sitting half upright. The room spun around him, and he had to put a hand down to keep his balance. He frowned, trying to get his bearings. He was lying on a couch. Beside him, a woman was curled up in an armchair, her eyes closed. Lamplight gilded the surface of her hair to a honeyed gold. An overwhelming sense of contentment flowed through him, warm and right. He reached over, cupping her cheek in his hand. "I've missed you, Nora."

The woman sat upright in the chair, leaning away from him, holding her hand to her face where he had touched her. "No. I'm sorry. My name is Rachel."

Michael blinked, and he saw her clearly. "Of course." He let his hand drop and cleared his throat, looking away. "We made it to the cabin."

"Yes." Faint red flushed her cheeks, but she lowered her hand and adopted a brisk, efficient manner. "I cleaned your wound. Let me see how it looks now."

Smooth fingers explored his scalp. He might have enjoyed her touch if he hadn't felt such a fool. Actually, he enjoyed it anyway. He put his hand up and felt the bandage across his temple. "Will I live, Doc?"

"It was only a graze. I think you'll survive."

"Thank you for bandaging me." His fingers traced the bandage. "Neatly done. Like a professional."

Rachel looked down at her hands. "It was

just like that time with the little girl. My hands just knew what to do."

She looked so lost, sitting there. Michael started to get up, swinging his legs off the couch. Rachel pressed her hand against his shoulder for a moment. "Don't get up. You lost a lot of blood. You need to take things easy."

"How long have I been out?"

"An hour or two."

"No sound of any cars in the area?"

"No. It's been quiet. It's been snowing since we came, and our tracks are already covered up."

"I think we're safe, then. If that man hasn't tracked us here by now, I doubt he will. This cabin isn't easy to find. It's off-the-grid. No electricity. Trouble is, no cell reception, either. I have no idea what's going on in the outside world."

An old metal coffeepot sat on top of the woodstove. Rachel poured out steaming coffee into a pair of thick ceramic mugs. She put one scoop of sugar into one of the mugs, from the battered old tin Michael had kept in the kitchen, and handed the mug to him. Then she settled back down in the armchair by the fire, putting her own mug on a side table and curling her legs up under her again. Even though she had stopped touching her cheek, her color was still high.

Interesting. She had fixed his coffee exactly the way he liked it without even asking. Michael considered pointing this out, but decided against it. Rachel clearly had other things on her mind.

She fixed her eyes on a level with his chin, avoiding direct eye contact. "You said going to the hospital would…be dangerous for you."

He had phrased it a lot stronger than that. Maybe she didn't like to think of anything happening to him? Maybe she still cared, just a little.

The coffee was strong and hot, clearing his mind wonderfully. He drained the mug and put it down on the side table. "Think it through. You have a driver's license, a social security card, all the paperwork you need to hold down a job. You couldn't have gotten all that on your own without help. Someone set you up with a new identity."

"Perhaps I got them in the ordinary way, as people normally do." Rachel cradled her own mug as though seeking its warmth, though the room was now at a comfortable temperature.

"Or perhaps I am telling the truth and you are Nora Stewart. In which case, someone had the paperwork ready when you were admitted to that hospital after the *accident*. That's why I can't go back there with you. If they find out I was helping you get out of town, I'd be a target, too. I can't help you and watch my back at the same time."

Rachel frowned into the black depths of her mug. "If you really are afraid to be seen with me, why were you standing outside the café, staring at me when I first saw you?"

"When I got to town, I didn't realize what was going on. I couldn't make sense of what had happened. It was totally against your nature to walk out without even leaving a note. You've—Nora has always been one of those people who puts others first. I knew there was no way you'd abandon your life. Not unless something had happened. But when I got to Sleepy Cove, I didn't realize there was a conspiracy to trap you there." His voice went lower. "I didn't realize you had forgotten me."

She shifted, looking away toward the fire.

Too much, too soon. Dial it back, Sullivan. "I tracked you down by going through reports on women checked in to hospitals. I was looking everywhere by that point. It took me months to go through all the files. I don't think anyone could have found you unless they were really looking hard. Someone went to a lot of trouble to hide you in that little town."

Rachel sighed. "Again with that conspiracy theory of yours."

He squinted at her. Sitting on the other side of the lamp made it hard to see her expression. But her tone made it clear what she thought about this. "So who do you think abducted you? And why? Or do you think it was just some random attack?"

"Well, that does happen," she said defensively. "I can't help wondering if there's a possibility that it's all a misunderstanding, people mistaking me for this Nora woman. First you, then those men in the van."

Michael had seen this kind of denial before. People would cling to any rationalization, no matter how improbable, if it kept them from facing an unpalatable truth. Gently, he said, "I know you don't want to talk about this. But people are trying to use you for their own ends."

"I know." Her voice had dropped until it was almost a whisper. "I know the most likely scenario is that they were after me. But I still cannot make sense of any of this. You keep telling me I'm someone else, but I sure don't *feel* like some kind of fancy doctor. I'm just me, Rachel."

"If we can find out what they want from you, that could give us enough information to plan how to keep you safe."

Rachel busied herself adding another log to the stove, though the fire was burning well already. Then she sat back, dusting her hands. "Well, I guess once I get back to Sleepy Cove, I'll report the whole affair to Tony. He'll know what to do."

"Tony? You mean that potbellied sheriff? He'd be completely out of his depth. That's assuming he's not in league with your enemies."

"I trust Tony," Rachel said firmly. "He only wants what is best for me."

"I'll report this to the state police," Michael decided.

"Will you? How? I thought you said there was no cell phone reception here."

"There's a small town a few miles away. Not much more than a gas station and a couple of stores, but I can get a cell phone signal and make calls from the coffee shop there."

"Does it have a doctor? You really should have that head wound checked out."

"I'm fine." Michael leaned forward. "But right now all we've got is a woman with memory problems and a couple of thugs who wanted to grab her off the street. There's nothing to connect the two. We need more evidence."

"How do you propose we get it? If the bad guys are not in Sleepy Cove, then we've got the whole world to choose from."

"I think we can narrow the possibilities down to one. You have no family, your parents are dead and you were an only child. I know you kept in touch with friends from college, but it's all been long-distance since you came out to Oregon and started your job. That's been the focus of your life in the last few years."

"Sounds lonely," Rachel couldn't help saying.

But Michael shook his head. "No. You loved the work." He suppressed a smile. "I made sure to distract you when you weren't working."

Rachel smiled, a little bleakly, but Michael had gone back to staring into the fireplace. "I know you liked your job when you first started there. Very secret, some new wonder drug with great potential. There were drug trials, and everything was looking promising. Then Dr. Vance—the CEO—made some personnel changes. You weren't very happy about the situation. I had the impression the new staff was trying to change how the place was run.

And then—something went wrong. I think Vance was pressuring you to fudge some of the data. That's just a guess, based on what I know of Vance."

"And you don't think Nora would have gone along with him if he wanted to fake evidence."

"Never," he said flatly. "You wanted to help people. Vance wanted success at any price."

"You don't like the man."

"No, I don't. In my estimation, Vance is an adult version of a spoiled brat. Incapable of seeing anyone else's point of view. If an obstacle was blocking his path, he'd sweep it out of the way in the fastest manner possible, ethical or not. The end justifies the means, as far as he is concerned. He'd be perfectly capable of kidnapping you and brainwashing you." Absently, Michael tapped his fingers against the coffee mug. "Vance must be involved at some level—it's the only reason I can see for having you taken away but not killed. He couldn't be sure that he might not need the brilliant Dr. S and her amazing mind again."

"So you want to investigate Vance?"

"Vance and his company. If we go to that coffee shop tomorrow, I can check in with my office and see if there's anything on the web about Vance's company. I keep thinking something must have changed recently, or why pick you up."

"Perhaps it was you showing up that panicked this Vance man. Though I don't know how he'd know about it. Certainly no one in Sleepy Cove would have told him."

Michael didn't bother to challenge that. He switched his attention to the fire. Casually, he added, "And I was going to suggest you could go with me to Portland. To see that doctor I told you about."

Out of the corner of his eye, he saw her hands grip each other so tightly that her knuckles stood out. "That's too far. I need to return to Sleepy Cove."

"I could take you there afterward, maybe. If we get the state police involved, it might make the plotters hesitate." He hated the idea, but neither could he keep her here if she was bound and determined to go back. He had to find a way to persuade her to *want* to change. Maybe Parker could help.

"I thought you didn't want people to link the two of us together."

"I don't. But I'm not letting you go back there otherwise."

She sat up straight in her chair. "I can make

my own decisions. You don't *let* me do anything."

Despite his frustration, he smiled. "That
sounds like the old Nora I knew."

Rachel met his eyes then, and for a moment
Michael felt the connection between them like
a live wire. He leaned forward. Was she starting to remember?

But then Rachel looked away. "And that's
another thing. This doctor friend of yours.
Suppose he thinks I'm this Nora woman, as
well. I'm not saying I agree with the idea. Just
indulge me in a hypothetical discussion here.
What if he tells me I can somehow revert to
being her again? Why should I? I like my life
as it is now. Not—" she waved a hand "—not
the phobias. I want to walk where I choose
and not feel afraid. But I love living in Sleepy
Cove. All my friends are there."

"Your enemies are there, too. Until you can
tell one from the other, Sleepy Cove is the last
place you should go."

He wanted so badly to tell her about Nora,
to explain how fully she had loved her life.
How they had planned to get married. But
the words stuck in his throat. Rachel trusted
him—but not enough for that. Not yet. "Just
talk to Parker. Will you do that?"

"I'll think about it."

Michael bit off an impatient response. Rachel was poised on the edge of the chair, ready to bolt up if he made the wrong move. "We can't go back. Not until we know more. You can't even begin to know how to defend yourself, and I don't want them to see us together unless there's no other choice. You are safe here for now. We have a chance to form a plan of our own instead of reacting blindly. Do you remember anything the kidnappers said?"

"They didn't say much." Rachel scrunched her forehead in an effort to recall specifics. "They were ordered to take me somewhere. And…some man gave them a drug that would knock me out. A specific dosage. The man didn't want them to give me too much of it."

"So whoever's behind this has some knowledge of drugs, which could point to Vance. And whatever's going on is not based in Sleepy Cove. The decisions are being made somewhere else. Maybe I can check in with my boss, see if there have been any other attempted abductions in the area lately."

"Tony would know. He knows everything that goes on in the area."

"I'm sorry, but I don't think a small-town

sheriff is going to be the right person to handle a situation like this."

Rachel folded her arms. That stubborn lift of her chin was a gesture so familiar, so like the old Nora, that it made him want to smile, despite the seriousness of the moment.

"Nora—" She made a restive movement, and he stopped. "I will stop calling you that if it bothers you, but this is not a problem you can solve by going back to your safe little existence and hiding. The only way to feel safe is to go forward, not back."

Rachel got up and looked out the window at the falling snow. "We can't stay here forever."

"We can stay for a week or two, if we must. I've stocked up on food, and there's a good supply of firewood in the shed."

"A week!" She wrenched the curtains closed in one swift motion.

"Please don't take your frustration out on the furnishings," Michael said mildly.

Rachel turned back to face him. "I can't help it. I need to go back to Sleepy Cove. That's the only place I know I'll be safe."

"It's not safe any longer."

Rachel did not move. The lamp outlined her hair in gold. She looked more beautiful than he remembered, but there was a weariness in her stance, the way she hunched her shoulders, that he had never seen in his Nora. "You might be right. I still need to go back."

Michael sighed. "I don't want to pressure you. How's this for a compromise. After you talk to the doctor, I'll take you back. Will that work?"

She shook her head, but the response was not as quick this time. She was at least considering it. "And I need to call my friends, let them know where I am."

"No. No one can know your location."

"But they'll be worried! I need to at least tell them I'm all right."

"Well…" Michael hated the idea of taking Rachel to the small town. He wanted her safely under Parker's supervision, where she could get the proper medical care.

Rachel came back and sat in the armchair. "That's my deal. If you get me to a place where I can telephone my friends, then I will go to see this doctor with you. And then you'll take me back to Sleepy Cove."

"If that's the best deal I'm going to get, I'll take it."

"It is."

"Yes, ma'am." He gestured at the window.

"It's getting dark, and I don't want to risk driving until I've had a chance to rest."

Rachel hesitated. "That's a good point. And you need food, too. You lost a fair amount of blood, and your body needs time to heal."

"So can we wait until morning?" Rachel still looked doubtful. Michael reached out his hand and laid it over hers. "Please."

Rachel looked down, frowning. "Okay." Red embarrassment tinged her cheeks, and she withdrew her hand from under his as if the contact burned her, but she nodded. "We'll go tomorrow."

What a fool I am. But Rachel could not help it. Every time he touched her, she was distracted. She had to get her reaction to him under control. She fingered the cuff of her sweatshirt. "Thank you for the clothing."

"Anything I have, it's yours," he said softly. Rachel looked up, and her eyes met his for a moment that lengthened into a slice of eternity. The sincerity in his blue eyes warmed her more than the fire ever could.

Rachel's lips parted. She wanted to say something, but no words came. It was hard enough just to think straight when he looked at her with such intensity. Her emotions whirled about her in dizzying confusion, like snow-flakes in a blizzard. She looked away.

Michael sighed, so softly that she almost didn't catch it. "Don't worry about Parker. He won't push you. Neither will I. If you're not ready to accept being Nora, I'll wait." He got to his feet, a bit unsteadily. "I want to look around, make sure everything is all right."

Rachel frowned at the door he'd shut behind him. Michael was obsessed with that Nora woman. The thought was like a hovering gnat, irritating and impossible to shoo away. *Don't be such a fool.* It was nothing to her if Michael wanted to chase a fantasy rather than notice the flesh-and-blood woman in front of him. Her fingers covered her other hand, where he had touched her. There was a connection between them, between Michael and *her*, Rachel. Why couldn't he accept her as she was?

Michael came back in, stomping the snow off his boots. "Everything looks all right out-side. No sign of any intruders, and the snow's covered our tracks. I've got enough blankets to keep warm here tonight. There's only one bedroom, I'm afraid, but it's got several blan-kets. Keep the door open a crack and the stove will heat the room."

She looked up at him, suddenly aware of

how close he was. "I never said thank you for rescuing me from the van." She gave a huff of a laugh. "It sounds so inadequate. A few words. But I really am grateful."

He took her hand, gave it a gentle squeeze. "I will do anything in my power to keep you safe. Remember that." He held her hand a moment longer and she looked up at him. In the dim light from the lamp, Rachel could not read Michael's expression, but the silence between them came alive with her awareness of how close he stood to her, his warmth and strength.

Rachel swallowed. Michael dropped her hand. "Well, good night."

"Good night," she whispered.

That night, she dreamed of Michael again. Walking down a lane hand in hand between tall trees bright with autumn colors. Then stargazing, wrapped up in blankets side by side, gazing in delight as meteors streaked across the darkness above them. Michael's voice warm in her ear, whispering to her. She still couldn't hear what he said, but it felt so good to have his arms around her, warm and secure. She was filled with contentment so completely there was no room in her for fear. But what had he been saying to her? She felt like an outsider, looking through a window into someone else's home where she did not belong.

Then the dream changed to her dancing with Michael at a fancy party, her hair up and wearing a glittering dress, Michael with his hair cut short, wearing a tux. Smiling down at her. Putting a ring on her finger.

She woke up in the night, sat bolt upright.

The mountain silence was absolute. Rachel could hear nothing outside, not even the wind. From the main room, she heard the faint rustle of a log settling in the woodstove and Michael's regular, even breathing.

Rachel touched the bare skin on the third finger of her left hand and missed the weight of the diamond there. It had been so real…

According to the battery-powered alarm clock on the dresser, she had woken in the middle of the night. She went to the bedroom window and looked out. It had stopped snowing. A crescent moon showed faintly through the thin layer of clouds. The snow lay perfectly white and smooth against the backdrop of the dark woods. The night was perfectly silent.

Rachel had never felt more alone in her life.

Michael was just in the next room, sleeping on the couch. She could go to him, touch his hand, wake him up. Sit with him until she felt a flicker of warmth inside her again.

But no. She could never do that. He wanted Nora. With an intensity that frightened her, Rachel wanted to go back to the warmth and companionship she had felt in her dream. But that's all it had been—a dream. Michael was in love with someone else. Someone she didn't know how to be.

SIX

The next day, the clouds hung low overhead, dark and threatening. As they headed down the trail to the car, Michael frowned up at the sky. "I don't like the look of that. Once we finish your call, I want to get on the road to Portland right away. If it starts snowing heavily, we'll never make it over the pass."

Michael had found a razor somewhere and shaved off the stubble from his jaw. He looked good. Too good. Rachel kept her eyes on the ground and focused on stepping in his footsteps through the snow.

It didn't help that she had to sit next to him in an SUV that was suddenly way too small. Rachel was overwhelmingly aware of how close he was to her. A faint scent teased her, something subtle that was woodsy with a note of spice. She could not identify the mixture.

She sniffed. "What is that smell? It's familiar somehow."

Michael gave her a sidelong glance and then went back to watching the road. "My aftershave. A present from—a good friend."

He did not specify further. There was no need. "She had good taste," Rachel said politely. Then she turned her head away. Focused on not noticing how intimate it felt to be alone with him in this car. How easy it would be to reach out and touch his hand.

The drive only lasted half an hour, but the time stretched out until it felt much longer. Tongue-tied and awkward, Rachel could not come up with anything to say. Nothing that would be safe to say. Nothing that wouldn't reveal her growing attraction to him.

Michael was silent, as well. She darted a sideways glance at him. He was intent on the road, a faint suggestion of a frown line between his eyebrows.

Town was far too grand a name for their destination. A more apt description would be to call the place a haphazard collection of stores huddled together along a riverbank. Michael parked the car near the bridge that crossed the river. "This way." He led her to a tiny coffee shop tucked in between the gas station and a hardware store.

The coffee shop was full of warmth and the smell of fresh baked bread. It would have been a cozy spot if it weren't for the blare of the television over the counter, playing a noisy game show. They settled into a booth by the front window. Rachel gratefully wrapped her fingers around the mug of hot chocolate he bought her as Michael scanned his phone. "Do you see anything?"

Michael shook his head, his eyes still running down the article on his phone. "There's an article in a business magazine about how Vance's company is heavily reliant on investors to keep the lights on. Vance keeps putting out announcements about being on the verge of a breakthrough but no concrete details yet."

"That hardly seems like something that would warrant kidnapping me."

Michael drummed his fingers against the Formica tabletop. "Maybe it was something that you said or did that triggered an alarm on someone's part."

Rachel shook her head. "I don't think I did anything extraordinary recently. The only change in my life was meeting you."

"We were seen together twice—at your café

and on the street after the little girl fell down. I don't think that should have been enough to cause such an extreme reaction as grabbing you off the street." He shook his head, as though clearing his thoughts. "Have you finished your chocolate? Good. Let's go outside. It's colder, but quieter than this place."

A few stray snowflakes spiraled down as Rachel followed him to the river's edge. Michael said, "I need to call my boss, check on some things. I'll come back when I'm finished." He went a few paces off, giving her privacy to place her own call.

Corrie picked up the phone on the first ring. "Rachel! Where are you? Are you all right? I've been so worried!"

Rachel took a breath, trying to think of how to tell Corrie everything that had happened without throwing her friend's protective nature into overdrive. "I am all right—at least, I am all right now. Don't worry about me. Some men tried to kidnap me, but a friend came by—" she supposed she could describe Michael as such "—and he helped me frighten them off. I'm safe now."

Corrie did not sound appeased. If anything, her voice sharpened into suspicion. "What do you mean a friend helped you? What friend? I know all your friends, and they're right here."

"Corrie, I can give you the whole story later, all right? I'm fine, that's the main thing." It was cold, standing there, even with the warm jacket Michael had brought for her. The snow was falling more steadily now. Rachel blinked a snowflake out of her eye.

The last thing she wanted to do was give a detailed explanation of how she had met Michael. The story sounded implausible, and Michael's story was more unbelievable still. She needed time to find a way to explain the situation that would make sense.

Besides, if Michael was right and someone in town had set up this new persona for her, she did not want word to get back to them. So she temporized. "I did have friends before I came to Sleepy Cove, you know. This man is a friend from my past. He helped me get away from the men who were threatening me. I can't go into the details now. I'll explain once I'm back. Anyway, I just wanted you to know that I am safe. Don't worry about me. I'm not coming back to Sleepy Cove today but I will be back soon. I'm sorry I'm going to miss work."

Corrie said, "I don't understand what is going on. Where are you now?"

"I'm not quite sure. I'm in a small town, and—" Michael was back, putting his hand over the cell phone for a moment and shaking his head.

"What was that? I didn't catch what you said."

"I'm sorry, the cell phone reception here is rather bad," Rachel said. "I will be back in Sleepy Cove very soon. Don't worry."

Corrie said to someone, "Here, you talk to her. She won't tell me anything."

Tony's voice came on the line. "Rach, are you okay? Where are you? Tell me where you are and I'll come pick you up."

"I'm fine. You don't need to pick me up. I've got a ride back to town."

Michael gestured with his hand, indicating that she should finish talking. Rachel said, "I have to go now. You take care, and I will be back as soon as I can. I'll call you later." She ended the call before Tony could ask anything more.

Michael took Rachel by the arm and bent down to say, low, "Get in the car. Now." As soon as she shut the door, Michael started the car and swung into the street.

"What's wrong? I thought you were going to phone the state police."

"Two men," Michael said tensely. "Behind us. They just got into a white van."

Rachel twisted around. "I can't tell if it's fol-lowing us or not." Snow was falling so thickly it was difficult to see the road. Even at the fast-est setting, the rear wipers barely cleaned the window before snow covered it again.

"Turn off your cell phone. I don't think they can get a ping, but I want to be sure."

He rounded the corner. Rachel looked back. "They're getting closer."

Michael tossed his cell phone to Rachel. "See if you can call 911."

Rachel fumbled with the buttons. "I can't get a signal."

"I was afraid of that." The road was still climbing. "I want to find out who these men are and what they want, but not now. For all I know, they've already called for backup. Try to get a license plate."

Rachel rolled down her window, letting in a whirl of cold air, and stuck her head out. She ducked back in, rolling up the window again. "They're too far back for me to see details." She shivered.

Michael flicked on the heater. "All right. I'm going to lose them." He swerved off onto a side road, a Forest Service dirt track, rough and deeply rutted. The SUV splashed through a mud puddle. Michael wrestled with the steering wheel. "Are they still following?"

"Yes. But they've slowed down. I don't think their van has four-wheel drive."

"That's what I was counting on." He skidded around a corner, still accelerating. Mud and slush splattered everywhere. Rachel clung to the door frame and braced herself. The road sloped upward, a long straight stretch. Michael floored it. "Let's hope we can get up this hill. I studied a map of the roads around here. If I'm right, it connects to a side trail that will take us back to the main highway."

"They can't make it!" Behind them, the white van was slipping, sliding back down the hill. "They can't get enough traction."

"Perfect," Michael said with satisfaction. They rounded a corner, the wind slackening as the hill sheltered them from the force of the storm. "I don't think we're going to make it over the pass. We'll have to head back to the cabin. As soon as the storm blows over, we can head out and see Parker. And he will help you." His hand descended on hers with a quick firm grip. "I promise."

The snow piled up. Two days, three days, four. The cabin was well stocked with supplies, and there was more than enough wood to keep the cabin warm despite the snow. Yet Rachel could not relax completely.

Michael had answered all her questions about Nora—except the one question she hadn't dared to ask. What exactly was the relationship between him and Nora? He'd taken leave from his job, put his life on hold, walked away from all other obligations to track the woman down. All he said was they had been close. How close?

The question mattered.

A lot.

She was attracted to Michael. A part of her was beginning to suspect that his wild story about her might be the truth. But no matter how convincing the evidence, she didn't *feel* like Nora Stewart. If he looked at Rachel with love, would it be love for her—or someone else?

On the fourth day, Rachel woke to a beautiful crisp, clear day. When she stepped onto the porch, she paused to take in the vivid scenery. Deep green trees, sparkling white snow and overarching deep blue sky. Snow was piled up in drifts several feet high, a sea of unbroken white. The sun shone down, but it was still very cold. Her breath showed as a white plume in front of her.

Michael came to stand beside her. "No way we're getting through that, not until the weather warms up enough to soften the snow. After breakfast, I think it's time you learned how to fire a gun."

"Wait—where did that come from?" Rachel turned to look at Michael. In a deep blue sweater, with his hair neatly brushed back and the sun gilding his jawline, he looked more like a male model than a marshal. It gave her a pang, somewhere in the region of her heart. She steeled herself to concentrate on the topic at hand. "How did you jump from going back to firearms?"

"I have no intention of letting someone take a shot at you ever again," Michael said, matter-of-fact. "But I want you to be prepared for any eventuality."

He took Rachel out behind the cabin to a clearing not far from where the car was parked.

The gun was surprisingly heavy for its size. She was glad of the gloves that Michael provided; the cold seemed to radiate from the smooth gray metal. She aimed carefully, but instead of the pine cone she was aiming at, she clipped the edge of the tree trunk.

"I'm awful," Rachel said ruefully.

"That doesn't matter," Michael said. "Not as much as you think. If you shoot at people, they are not likely to stand still long enough to verify whether you know what you're doing or not."

"Here." His hands touched her shoulders briefly, adjusting her position. "Widen your stance and try again."

In general, Rachel did not like being touched even by people she knew well, such as Corrie. But Michael was different. She welcomed his touch. Indeed, she wouldn't have minded if his hand lingered on hers, gave additional pressure or a friendly squeeze.

But Michael took care, it seemed to her, not to touch her more than he had to. Very brief touches on the shoulder, moving her arms. He released her as soon as he could. Rachel was not sure if he was being restrained because he was not interested in her or if he was trying to be a gentleman.

When he moved away, her skin prickled, sensitized to the feel of his warm calloused fingertips. Missing his touch.

Michael looked down at her and smiled quizzically. "You have the oddest expression on your face. What are you thinking?"

Rachel made a show of stomping her feet against the snow. "My feet are cold. I need to move around a bit to warm up."

"All right," Michael said. "I think we've subdued the pine tree population for now. You go inside and get warm. I'll get some more wood for the fireplace and meet you back at the cabin."

Rachel watched him walk away, kicking snow to widen the path to the woodshed. For some reason, for no reason, she smiled. When had she stopped feeling anxious about going back to Sleepy Cove? She couldn't remember.

Even if she could not claim Michael as her own, she had been happy here with him. They didn't have much time left for her to find the answers she needed. A spirit of mischief filled her. Perhaps there was a way she could break through his reserve, after all.

Michael stomped back up to the cabin, carrying a load of wood. The snowball arched down and hit him on the forehead, scattering loose snow down his sweater. "Hey!" He dropped the wood and grinned at her. "Now you're in trouble."

The battle was brief, but glorious. Rachel pinned him behind a pine tree, certain that victory was hers. But he ducked and threw a curveball that she had to jump back to avoid. Her foot slipped and suddenly she was flat on her back in the soft snow, sputtering with laughter. "Very sneaky."

Michael crouched over Rachel with his hands on either side of her, his light eyes glimmering with amusement. Then his expression deepened into something more serious. His eyes lingered on her lips, and for a wild moment she thought he meant to kiss her.

Rachel caught her breath, lips parted. She wasn't sure what she should do. She had thought she was ready for this moment, certain she wanted to be closer to him. And yet, right now she felt off balance and teetering on the edge of a precipice. The lightest touch and she'd fall. Hard.

One corner of his mouth twitched. "Do you know the penalty for assaulting a US marshal, young lady?"

"I'm not afraid." She tried to wriggle her way out from under him, but she was trapped. "Do your worst." Then, with belated caution, "Wait. What *is* the penalty?"

Michael leaned down until his breath tickled her ear. "This." He raised his head, his eyes sparkling, and dropped a soft fistful of snow directly on her face.

Rachel sputtered and twisted her head from side to side to shake the snow out of her eyes. Michael got to his feet and helped her up, brushing snow off her back. "If you're so eager to do something, come help me carry the wood." He dumped a log into her arms and laughed. She had never heard him laugh before. It made him sound years younger. "I'll race you back to the cabin." He grabbed the rest of the wood and started off down the trail.

"No fair! You have a head start."

But she won anyway. She suspected he'd let her win. She was laughing, too, when they came in. Then she changed into dry clothes while he cooked. They ate before the fire in a companionable silence, Michael sitting on the couch and Rachel in her usual armchair.

Rachel put a pan of water on the stove to heat for washing before settling back in the chair. She looked up to find Michael watching her.

"Tired?"

"A bit," Rachel confessed. "But I was thinking. Tomorrow, the roads will be clear and we can go back."

"We can go *on*," Michael corrected gently. "You agreed to come to Portland with me. Or have you changed your mind?"

"No. Of course. We'll go on to Portland to see your doctor friend."

"I'd like to stop at Salem to file a report with the state police, as well. Until we can find out who's behind those men who tried to kidnap you, you're in danger."

"And then I'll go back to Sleepy Cove."

Idly, Michael tapped his fingers against the side table. "I don't think the answer is there. Yes, there's a person or a group of people there who are involved in keeping you in line—" Michael stifled Rachel's instinctive protest by adding hastily, "Not all of them, of course."

"Humph."

"I think we have to assume there is at least one person there who is against you. But the heart of the conspiracy must lie somewhere else, or there'd be no point in taking you away."

Michael leaned forward to poke at the logs inside the woodstove. The fire leaped up, highlighting the planes of his face and the deep V between his eyebrows as he frowned in concentration. Even when he wasn't looking at her, she could not keep from watching him. There was something about him that drew her like a magnet. The firelight sculpted his face, throwing into relief his high cheekbones and the faint laugh lines around his eyes.

As if he felt her gaze, Michael glanced up suddenly. His eyes met hers. "What is it?"

"Nothing," Rachel said, hastily turning her gaze to the fire. She could feel her cheeks heating up. "But I won't go around doubting all my friends. It's a betrayal of their trust."

"Most of them probably are innocent people going about their daily lives," Michael said amiably.

Rachel closed her eyes for a moment. She sensed Michael watching her, though she was careful not to look his way. These feelings she was developing toward him—they were too new, too uncertain. She was afraid that her eyes would betray the truth—that she was in over her head where Michael Sullivan was concerned. *Concentrate on the issue at hand.* "We've gone over this again and again. There are too many unknown variables for us to solve this equation."

"You still talk like a scientist, even if you don't think of yourself as one."

"I talk like a logical person, that's all."

"Nora used to talk like that. But she never refused to look fear in the face."

"Well, maybe that's why she's not around."

"There must be a connection somewhere." Michael went back to tapping his fingers on the side table. "No one bothered you until I showed up."

"Do you mind not making that noise? It's annoying."

Lost in his thoughts, Michael paid no attention. "They couldn't risk my triggering a return of your memory. That's the only answer I can come up with."

"Seriously. Stop drumming your fingers. It's getting on my nerves."

"If you started asking the wrong kinds of questions or showed signs of behaving like a scientist instead of a waitress, maybe someone got alarmed and sent the men in the van to take you away for more treatment."

Rachel leaned over and squeezed Michael's fingers together. He looked at her and blinked. "What?"

"We're not going to find the answer by wild speculation," Rachel said firmly. "Come help me with the dishes."

A slow grin spread across Michael's face. Rachel's pulse, a traitor to her common sense, jumped in response. "Good thing I like bossy women."

"For that, you can scrub the frying pan," Rachel said with mock severity.

"Yes, ma'am." Michael began to roll up his sleeves. "Lead me to it."

They washed the dishes in companionable silence. Rachel's awareness of Michael's physical proximity only increased in the close confines of the kitchen. He laid the last plate on the draining tray, then reached across to grab a dish towel from the drawer. He was so close that his arm brushed the back of her hand. Only a casual, brief contact of his skin sliding against hers, but she blushed at the intimacy of it. It was surprising a gesture so small could carry so much intensity. She took a step back.

Michael seemed unaffected. "Did I jostle you? My apologies."

"No, no, it was nothing." Rachel stumbled over the words. If he didn't feel the same way she did, there was nothing for it but to act casual. "My mind was wandering, that's all."

"I was just surprised that you jumped back. Have you noticed that you haven't been so nervy lately?"

Rachel stopped drying for a moment, surprised. "I haven't been paying any attention, but you're right. I haven't had any anxiety attacks or headaches in days." Honesty prompted her to add, "I still feel compelled to get back to Sleepy Cove. But it's not an overwhelming urge, as it was before. More like a nagging itch."

"More like conditioning," Michael said darkly. "Nora would have had a few choice words to say to that doctor of yours."

"I can't imagine telling Dr. Green off. You know, the more I learn about Nora, the less I feel as if I have anything in common with her. No matter how good I am at bandaging people or performing first aid." Rachel kept her head down, scrubbing the last plate with more force than it needed.

Michael leaned forward. He laid one finger under Rachel's cheek, gently turning her around so he could look her in the eye. "You are still *you*. You are more than your past, more than a collection of memories. You are kind and caring and go out of your way to help people who need you. Just like Nora. You stand by your friends, just as she would." His fingers wrapped around her hand and he gave her a gentle squeeze. "And you don't let me get away with anything without challenging it, not if you disagree."

His hand was so warm against her skin. It was an intimate touch, reaching past her barriers to the loneliness hidden within.

Rachel couldn't look at him. If she did, he

would surely see how much his opinion mattered to her. How much *he* mattered. "So… you're not disappointed?" She rinsed off the last dish and put it on the counter.

Michael took the plate. Rachel thought he was going to dry it, but he merely propped it against the wall out of the way. Then he leaned closer, lifting her chin. "Look at me," he said, very softly, and Rachel summoned up her courage and looked him in the eye. She could not identify the expression in those light blue eyes, but it sent warmth running through her body. Her heart began to pound faster.

"I'm not disappointed at all," he whispered. "There's nothing wrong with you as you are." Then his lips grazed hers.

His kiss was tentative, a gentle exploration. Sensations swirled around her, too intense to analyze. Shock, certainly, but also joy. An odd sense of familiarity and belonging, as if coming home after a long journey. And running beneath everything else, a foundation of certainty. This was right. Cautiously, she leaned forward and kissed him back, tentatively at first, then with growing confidence.

It was like being swept off her feet in the ocean. She lost her footing. All she knew, all she was aware of, was the reality of Michael:

his arms pulling her against him, the warmth of his body, the need to get closer to him.

Michael drew back, and those light blue eyes studied her carefully. "Should I apologize for doing that? I should warn you, I've never felt less sorry in my life."

"No." It would be easier to think clearly if her heart weren't pounding so loud. "No, there's nothing to apologize for."

Michael leaned forward and kissed her again, with slow deliberation and sweet thoroughness. His lips traced a path from her lips along her jawline to the sensitive spot just under her ear. He murmured, "I've missed you, Nora."

Rachel froze. Literally, it felt as if her whole body had turned to ice. She stepped back. Suddenly, she needed nothing more than distance between them.

Michael stretched out his hands. "Wait. Don't leave like this. I meant what I said. You are still *you*, to me. There's no difference."

Rachel headed for the bedroom door, eager to escape. But his voice stopped her before she could turn the doorknob. "Are you still going to come with me to Portland?"

Hand on the doorknob, clinging to it for support, Rachel turned around to face him. "I'll go with you in the morning to see this doctor. Then I'm going back to Sleepy Cove—where I belong. Good night."

And she closed the bedroom door quietly behind her.

The next day Rachel could not look Michael in the eye, focusing on cooking and cleaning instead. Breakfast was an awkward affair, which Rachel mostly spent looking out the window. The snow was melting finally, the icicles turning into downspouts of drips.

Michael put down his coffee mug on the side table with a dull thud that seemed to echo in the quiet cabin. "I think it's safe to go now. I'll chop some more wood and stack it in the woodshed. I want to leave the cabin the way it was."

As if nothing had changed. Rachel wanted to kiss him so badly she ached from it. One sign of tenderness on his part, and she would be sure that he wanted *her.* She said, "Then I'll clean up the cabin."

As she swept and straightened up, Rachel looked around. This was a place where she'd been happy. She'd enjoyed her time with Michael. But he had to learn to see her as herself, or they could never have a future together.

Too restless to sit still, she put on her jacket and stepped out. The sunshine was dazzling against the white snow, but the south wind blew warm against her cheek. Michael was out of sight, but she could hear the steady rhythm of an ax thudding against wood and the faint *drip, drip* of snow melting to disturb the silence.

A load of snow slid off a fir tree, revealing the dark green bough underneath. Rachel jumped. Why was she so nervous? She hadn't felt uneasy in days, but she did now. Suddenly, she was convinced that someone was out there. Watching her. But she couldn't see anyone.

Quickly now, she followed the path that Michael had made through the snow. If she could get to him, she would be safe.

The trail rounded a tree and she was in the woods. Rachel could only see a few feet in any direction. Her imagination supplied kidnappers behind every tree trunk, waiting to grab her.

This was absurd. She was *not* going to give in to unreasonable fear. All the same, she moved faster.

As she passed a gnarled dead tree, strong hands grabbed her, wrenching her off the trail.

Even as she drew breath to scream, a rough hand covered her mouth.

Then a familiar voice was saying, "Rach, are you okay?"

She blinked up at the man. "Tony?"

"We have to get out of here," Tony said. "You're in danger."

SEVEN

Tony hustled her off the trail and away through the snow between the trees.

"Tony, wait. Where are we going? It's all right. Michael isn't going to hurt me."

"That's what you think," Tony said grimly. "That man is a dangerous lunatic. I'm amazed you're still alive."

"What?" Rachel wasn't sure whether to laugh or cry. "You have it all wrong. Michael did not kidnap me. There were two men driving a van. They grabbed me off the street. Michael actually saved me."

Tony didn't slow his pace. His grip on her arm was so tight she couldn't break free. Rachel hung back, using her weight to slow him down. "Tony, if there's a problem, let me help. I can talk to Michael. He listens to me."

"Not a chance." They had reached the road. His police car was parked on the side, already pointing back downhill. Tony all but pushed Rachel into the passenger side of the car, slamming the door shut before running around to slide behind the steering wheel. He started the car and put it in gear before Rachel had time to protest.

As he guided the car around a pothole, Tony tossed a piece of paper into her lap. A newspaper clipping. "Here. Read this and tell me that man isn't dangerous."

Rachel scanned down the page. Words and phrases leaped out at her, but her brain scrambled to make sense of them. "Isolationist… Doomsday cult… Illegal arms dealer…"

She let the paper drop to her lap. "I don't understand," she said helplessly. "That can't be Michael." Fear tightened her throat. "It's a coincidence," she said loudly. Was she trying to convince Tony or herself?

"I know this is going to be hard for you to hear, but the facts are all there. There was a group that used to hide out in the mountains, stockpiling illegal weapons and even making bombs. The US marshals got involved—they shut the group down—but apparently there was evidence linking this man Sullivan to the group. The state police got a tip that he's gone back to his old isolationist ways. He's a danger to society."

"That's absurd! He's the furthest thing from—"

"Rachel. Seriously. Think about it. Why is he hiding in a primitive cabin that doesn't even have electricity—in the middle of winter—if he doesn't have something to hide?"

She couldn't tell Tony that Michael suspected the sheriff of being part of some conspiracy against her. The story still sounded completely out there, even if she really were this Nora Stewart person. "I'm sure he would be able to explain everything if you'd just talk to him," she said weakly.

"Not me," Tony said. "My job was to get you out of there safely. The state police will take him in for questioning."

Rachel felt sick to her stomach. She trusted Tony the way she trusted the sun to rise in the east. He wouldn't lie to her. But it was beyond comprehension that Michael would be up to something illegal.

"There must be some mistake," she said desperately. "He rescued me from the men in the van who kidnapped me. He didn't have to do that."

"He probably arranged for the men to kidnap

you." Tony's voice was somber. He was taking no pleasure in this. "Then he'd look like a hero when he rescued you. I mean, c'mon. Why else would anyone want to kidnap you?"

"Well, no, that didn't make sense to me, either." It all rang true. "But I saw Michael get shot. He was bleeding a lot from a head wound."

Tony snorted. "He could have nicked his head with a knife to make it bleed."

"I know the difference between a knife wound and the graze left by a bullet," Rachel said dryly.

"I think you've been reading too many thrillers." Tony reached over, patting her shoulder. "You're a waitress, not a doctor."

Rachel grasped at this truth like a lifeline tossed to a drowning woman. She *was* a waitress. She was not this wonder doctor Michael had spoken of so fondly. She had to hold on to what she knew to be the truth. Hold on to who she was. Tony must be right.

And yet… Rachel so badly wanted Tony to be wrong. Maybe she really was going crazy.

Rachel tried to read the printout again, but tears blurred her eyes. She would have to read it later. She gazed out the window surreptitiously wiping her eyes so Tony wouldn't notice. They turned onto the highway. Tony slowed the car and rolled down the window. A man with grizzled gray hair wearing a SWAT jacket came over. Tony said, "He's chopping wood in the clearing beyond the cabin. He didn't see us."

The man nodded. "Leave him to us."

"Right," Tony said. He rolled up his window and drove on down the road.

Rachel twisted around in the seat to look back. "Tony... Those men. Are they going to storm the place? They might hurt Michael." *They might kill him. No. Oh, dear Lord, please no.* "We have to go back!"

"Not a chance." Tony accelerated down the highway. "My job is to get you back to where you'll be safe. Don't worry about Sullivan. If he's got any sense, he'll let them take him quietly."

The trees outside the window blurred into a solid wall of green. Or was that the tears that she couldn't stop from falling? Rachel closed her eyes and sent a brief heartfelt prayer. *Lord, I have no idea what is going on. But keep Michael safe. I need him safe.*

At the police station, Rachel faced what felt like an endless barrage of questions. She explained what had happened as clearly as she could. The men in the white van. Michael rescuing her.

When Rachel mentioned Michael's being a US marshal, the policeman's eyebrows rose almost to his hairline. Rachel hurried to lay stress on all the ways Michael had helped her. Taking her to the cabin for her own safety. Driving her to town to call Corrie so she'd know Rachel was all right. Letting her decide when to go to Portland.

Rachel made no mention of Dr. Parker by name, just saying that Michael had wanted to take her to Portland for more treatment. She wasn't even sure if there really was a Dr. Parker. She wasn't sure of anything by this point, except that Michael was in trouble.

When the police questioned her, Dr. Green insisted on being in the room with her the whole time, her arms crossed, listening to Rachel's story with a frown. She even stayed by Rachel's side when the police doctor examined her. The police doctor had looked annoyed at her pushiness, but he said nothing, merely writing down his notes. Finally, the questions came to an end. Rachel leaned back in her chair, closing her eyes. The fluorescent lights in this tiny room shone too brightly. The light stabbed into her eyes. Weariness dragged at Rachel's bones.

Dr. Green laid her hand on Rachel's shoulder. "You must be exhausted after all these questions. Let's go to my office. I have your medicine ready, and we'll have a brief hypnosis session for your anxiety."

"Actually, I feel all right," Rachel said. "I'm just tired. I don't need a session just now. Thank you." All she wanted was to go home and shut the world out. No one would tell her anything about what had happened to Michael. Could she find out on the internet? There must be some information on the police scanners, surely? The uncertainty tightened in her gut, the old familiar fear. Except this time it was not for herself.

"Well, come by and I'll give you your medication. You have missed a couple days. That's not good for you." The doctor's fingers tightened on Rachel's shoulder like a claw.

Gently, Rachel shrugged Dr. Green's hand away. "I feel much better without the medication. I haven't had a headache in days, and I'm much less anxious, too. I was thinking it might be time to stop taking the pills."

"That is not your decision to make," Dr. Green said sharply.

The police doctor looked up from his notes and frowned. "Actually, it is. So long as she is of sound mind and mentally capable of making an informed decision."

An angry flush bloomed on Dr. Green's sallow cheeks. Odd, that. It almost seemed as if Dr. Green were displeased to see her so improved. Rachel felt the old familiar urge to try to appease the woman. "Perhaps I can come by tomorrow to see about a hypnosis session."

"Very sensible," the police doctor said firmly. Dr. Green pressed her lips together, but she did not argue further.

Tony got to his feet. "I'll give you a ride home."

Rachel had hoped to just go to her apartment in peace, but Tony overruled her, calling Corrie to walk Rachel up the stairs. As she stepped inside, Rachel patted her pocket. "Where is that newspaper cutting?"

"What are you talking about?" Corrie asked.

"Tony gave it to me. It was about Michael's previous crimes."

"I would think you'd like to put all that behind you." Corrie tugged on her arm when Rachel started to turn back. "Come on. Tony will be at the station writing up his report. You shouldn't bother him now." Reluctantly, Rachel allowed Corrie to lead her away.

As soon as she was alone in her apartment, Rachel pulled out her phone. The state police would not give Rachel any information, since she was neither Michael's lawyer nor a family member.

Still grasping the phone, Rachel paced back and forth. She could only go ten steps in any direction. She had always thought her apartment was cozy. Now, it felt stifling. Frustrated, she turned to the internet.

There were articles on people who stockpiled illegal weapons and tried to live completely off-the-grid. While some of them merely wanted to be left alone to live in peace, there were other groups who believed in a variety of conspiracy theories. Rachel couldn't find any indication that any of these groups had been involved in kidnapping women, however.

Had Tony made an innocent mistake? Or was someone trying to make her think Michael was an outlaw when he was actually an honest man?

Lord, help me find a way out of this maze. Guide me on the path I should follow. I am lost in the wilderness.

She found several Michael Sullivans on social media, but none who identified themselves as a US marshal or as an isolationist. So she tried a search for Dr. Nora Stewart. This turned up a photograph.

The photo was small, and she could not enlarge it. The woman appeared to be the same height and size as Rachel. But it wasn't just her facial characteristics that made Nora unlike Rachel. There was something indefinable that was different about this woman. Nora had a confident smile. She held her head high and looked straight at the camera. This was the woman who was sure of her place in the world. She was nothing like Rachel.

The dress Nora was wearing was oddly familiar, though. At first, Rachel couldn't pin down why. Then she remembered. The dress from her dream that night in the cabin. Rachel did not possess a dress like this, but somehow she could almost remember wearing it. It was an unsettling feeling.

It took Rachel a moment to recognize the tall man next to Nora. Michael. He looked younger, smiling down at Nora. Carefree, the way he had been in her dreams. Nora had one hand on the man's arm, and the diamond ring on her left hand glittered.

The caption at the bottom of the picture read, *Dr. Nora Stewart and her fiancé, Michael Sullivan*.

Rachel read the sentence and then read it again. She felt chilled, as if she'd jumped into an ice bath. Why hadn't Michael told her he was going to marry Nora? He had kissed *her*. And Rachel had kissed him back.

It felt like cheating or something. Poaching another woman's fiancé. Except she *was* his fiancée—if she really was this Nora woman. Rachel put her hand on her forehead as if she could stop all the thoughts whirling around.

Facts. That's what she had to concentrate on.

Tony had been so sure Michael was a criminal. Nora had been engaged to Michael. Michael was in love with Nora. And Rachel could not completely believe that she was Nora.

But…the dress was familiar. She could almost remember wearing it. And the diamond ring on Nora's finger—how was it she knew what it looked like before she'd even seen the picture?

There was no evidence to connect Michael with anything criminal. This picture suggested Michael's story was true… But if his story was true, then someone had set her up. Taken away her identity. Stripped her of all her memories.

Michael had not struck her as a man who was anything but grounded in reality. He had rescued her from those thugs who had kidnapped her. He had been shot at. Those had been real bullets. He surely could not, would not have arranged that.

Rachel typed in a search for information about amnesia. There really were people who had disappeared and then been found later with a new identity and no memory of their past. Michael hadn't made that part up. If that were true…

Rachel put her hands over her eyes as if she could shut out the memories. All the facts added up on his side, but all the evidence on the other side was also convincing.

If this total stranger—who might not be a stranger at all—had been telling the truth, that meant everything in her life was based on falsehoods and everyone around her was lying to her.

Rachel went to the window and stared down at the alley. From this position, she could just see the spot where she had tripped and Michael had covered her. She stared at it as if it could stop the thoughts whirling through her mind faster and faster.

What she found most convincing was that

moment after Michael had grabbed her on the highway to stop her from stepping into the street, when she had seen his gun holster. He had been so sure that Rachel would know him. And hurt when she hadn't.

Rachel turned away from the window. She went into her bedroom and sat on the bed. Her old Bible lay on the nightstand. Her fingers traced the embossed letters on the cover, then flipped it open to read her name inscribed inside. *To Rachel, with all my love.* Her mother had given her this Bible on her eighteenth birthday. It was one of the few things that had survived the fire.

Was that the truth? Or was this merely a prop intended to convince her of a past that had never existed?

She leafed through the pages until she found the psalms.

O Lord, thou hast searched me, and known me. Thou knowest my downsitting and mine uprising, thou understandest my thought afar off. Thou compassest my path and my lying down, and art acquainted with all my ways.

Whether her memories were true or false, the words in this book endured. There was truth there. The Lord knew her even if she did not know herself.

Rachel couldn't sit still. Mechanically, she began tidying the apartment, as if cleaning her home could help her clear her mind. But when she went to hang up her jacket in the closet, paper crinkled inside a pocket. She stopped. Slowly, she drew out an old envelope.

Her heart leaped with joy. Michael's phone number.

The phone rang and rang and went to voice mail. "Michael? If you get this message, please call me back. I want to make sure you're all right."

There was still the other phone number, the doctor friend Michael had mentioned. Rachel looked online and verified that Gregory Parker was a psychiatrist in Portland. But the phone number on the website did not match the number that Michael had given her. Her spirits plummeted. Michael had lied to her.

No. She would call the number, anyway. Even if it was only the number of a pizza place, she had to know what the truth was.

The man answered on the second ring. "Parker."

"Hello." She fumbled, not sure what to say. She hadn't actually expected anyone to answer. "I was trying to get in touch with a friend of a friend. That is, I mean—" She was floundering. Must sound like an idiot. Well, she had nothing to lose by this point. "Are you a friend of Michael Sullivan?"

"Whom am I speaking with?"

"My name is Rachel Garrett. Michael gave me this number. He said it was the number of a friend of his. A doctor. I mean…"

"Yes, I am a doctor, and yes, I do have a friend named Michael Sullivan. Pardon my surprise. He doesn't usually give my personal cell phone number to people. I take it he felt you needed someone to talk to?"

"Well…it's just that Michael was concerned that my doctor was prescribing medication that perhaps wasn't as helpful as it could be. I have a problem. I was in a car accident and…" She stopped and then said in a rush, "Michael says I have lost my memory and don't remember who I am. He said I used to be a woman called Nora."

"Nora." The man's voice altered. "Yes. Michael told me about you. Please don't apologize for calling. I can't diagnose a problem over the phone, but if I can't help you, I can certainly refer you to someone who can. You don't need to be afraid of asking for help. Please understand that."

"I'm afraid that Michael wants me to go to

you for treatment so you can turn me back into Nora."

Dr. Parker said gently, "I've known Michael Sullivan a long time. He wouldn't tell you that if he didn't think treatment would help you."

"People keep telling me I need help," Rachel said forlornly. "But if Michael is telling the truth, then all my friends are lying to me."

"It's not always easy to separate truth from fiction. If people have been lying to you, inevitably they will slip up sooner or later. If you keep digging, you'll find the truth. If that's what you want to find."

Rachel transferred the phone to her other ear. Sweat made her hands slick. "Michael said you told him I had some kind of amnesia."

"A dissociative fugue, yes. But please understand that was only a guess. I can't make a definitive diagnosis without seeing you."

"I looked the condition up on the internet. Michael told me you mentioned Agatha Christie, but there are other cases. The most famous is Ansel Bourne." The words tumbled out of Rachel. This man probably knew all this already, but she couldn't seem to stop herself. It felt like a release, laying down a burden to share this with him. "He was a preacher from Rhode Island who traveled one day up to Providence. Except he ended up in Pennsylvania, where he began to work in a shop. No one who dealt with him thought anything was wrong. After two months, he knocked on his land-lord's door and asked, 'Where am I?' He had no idea why he wasn't in Providence or what had happened to him over the previous two months. Or there was Hannah Upp, who was a schoolteacher in Manhattan. She went out jogging and disappeared. For weeks, people claimed to have seen her around town. Even-tually she was found floating in the river by a Staten Island ferry captain. When they pulled her out of the water, she had no memory of where she'd been or how she'd been living. She worried about getting to her schoolroom so she could set up for the school term—which had already started three weeks before."

"Yes," Dr. Parker said patiently. "These are well-known cases."

"Well, that's where I have a problem." Ra-chel took a deep breath. "I noticed a pattern in these cases. All these people lost their iden-tity, disappeared and lived as someone else. Then eventually came back to their original self again. But…when they did, they lost all memory of who they'd been as the other iden-tity. Every scrap of memory, every joke shared with friends, every achievement or failure. All gone." Rachel's hand clenched around the piece of paper, crushing it. "Being Rachel is all I've ever known."

Dr. Parker said, "None of those cases involved a person who was being systematically drugged, as I believe you are. What has been done to you, as Michael described it, sounds more like a form of brainwashing. Not replacing your personality so much as repressing it. I think it is possible that you will just regain your old memories in time. And quite possibly you might well retain your current memories along with your old ones." His voice softened. "But of course, there are no guarantees. It's perfectly understandable if you are afraid. But you don't need to face the prospect alone."

"Thank you." Rachel's throat felt tight.

"Anxiety issues are among the most common issues people face these days. If someone is deliberately inducing this condition in you, then they have to be stopped. You can count on me to do whatever I can to help you."

Without warning, tears were brimming in her eyes, threatening to run down her cheeks in hot betrayal. Why was she upset? He was being helpful.

"Is Michael still in Sleepy Cove?" the doctor asked.

Rachel explained about the man in the van kidnapping her, Michael's rescue and then Tony taking her away. About Tony's accusations against Michael.

Dr. Parker said, "If the state police won't give you information, they won't tell me anything, either. But I can call Michael's boss. I used to serve with him and Michael back in the army. Lynch joined the Marshals after he got out, and then later Michael went to work for him. The police will listen to him."

"So he really is a marshal." Another truth. Enough of those and she could build a foundation for her life again. "And he was never in prison? Or…arrested for anything?"

There was a pause. Dr. Parker said gently, "Michael Sullivan is a good man. He's not a criminal."

Well, of course, his friend would say that. Even so, after she hung up with Dr. Parker, Rachel could not resist calling Michael one more time. The phone rang and rang again before she heard Michael's voice. "Hello. I can't come to the phone…"

"My phone is ringing again."

The police lieutenant, a portly man with a

sunburned face and cynical gray eyes, ignored this comment. Beside him, another man, with short-cropped dark hair and a salt-and-pepper mustache, opened his mouth to say something, but closed it again. He had been silent through most of the interview. The phone stopped ringing.

He was stuck in a windowless room with no indication of whether it was day or night. All Michael had to go by was how he felt, which was as if he had been stuck in this pokey room for days.

"So you admit you were involved with that isolationist group?"

"I infiltrated the group to get close to a suspect. That was last year. I haven't had any contact with anyone from the group since then. And no, I did not kidnap the woman. If you check with her, she will verify my story."

The lieutenant tapped his pen against the police report. "A woman on medication for mental health issues and, according to you, with memory problems? Not very convincing. You have a permit for that gun of yours?"

"I showed you my identification. If you contact my boss, he can verify that I am a US marshal."

"We've verified your prints match the ones

on file," the lieutenant said grudgingly. "But your boss is out of the office, and all anyone will tell us is that you've taken a leave of absence for personal reasons."

The quiet man added, "And your behavior doesn't fit with law enforcement guidelines. You found a woman in distress on the side of the road, and instead of taking her to a hospital, you isolated her with you in a remote cabin where she could not contact anyone if she needed help."

The police lieutenant frowned at the interruption. "Let's return to your activities. You shot the tires out of a van."

"After they took a shot at me. Yes."

The lieutenant leaned back in his chair, folding his arms and looking satisfied. Irritation raked down Michael's nerves. "*After* they took a shot at me. Self-defense." He stopped. Alienating this man further would only make his job harder. "The point is, there are a couple men out there who tried to kidnap the woman calling herself Rachel Garrett. We need to find them, see who's behind all this."

The lieutenant raised one eyebrow. "We?"

"*Some*one needs to find them."

Michael's phone, on the table between them,

began to ring again. "Sure you don't want me to answer that?"

The quiet man pressed the mute button on the phone. Blessed silence fell.

"Thank you," Michael said. "Though I would rather have answered it. She might need my help. I know how crazy the story sounds. But it's true. Rachel's not safe in that town."

The quiet man leaned forward, his dark eyes sharp. "Even you refer to her as Rachel Garrett instead of calling her by this doctor woman's name."

"I can't force her to accept her real identity," Michael snapped. "She needs a doctor's help to get her to see the truth."

"According to you, she's already being helped by a doctor."

"Not a good one. That woman keeps filling Rachel's head with lies until she doesn't know who to trust."

"Sounds to me like you want to do the same thing. The local sheriff, he says you've been stalking this Garrett woman all around town. He's got witnesses who will verify his story."

"I wasn't *stalking* her. Exactly. I just wanted to talk to her alone."

"Uh-huh. He seems to think there's some

evidence that you've got a problem with staying within the law."

"That's absurd."

"Probably," the quiet man agreed. "Looks like he got you mixed up with someone else. Doesn't make the rest of your story true. There is no sign of any mysterious van or any other man who could be a kidnapper, except for you."

The lieutenant snorted. "The whole story sounds crazy. Why would anyone go to all this trouble to kidnap a woman and brainwash her?"

"Because pharmaceuticals are a huge business. There are billions of dollars at stake here. People go to extreme lengths when there's this much money involved. Especially someone like Dr. Vance."

The quiet man's eyes narrowed. "Christopher Vance?"

The lieutenant said, "But the plain fact is, you have no proof. None at all."

"I know," Michael said. He opened his hands in frustration. "But that does not mean my story is wrong. I just need to get proof."

EIGHT

The next morning, Rachel went back to work. For once, she overruled Corrie's suggestion that she stay home and rest. She needed to return to normality.

Whatever that was.

Michael was gone, leaving her with nothing but questions. She craved security with eager desperation. Every certainty in her life was slipping away from her.

The Blue Whale Café was crowded. Rachel was kept busy all morning taking orders. She parried questions about her kidnapping, playing down the details as best she could. Making it sound like a college boy's prank.

Part of her mind saw these people as local residents going about their everyday lives, curious about the drama that had come into her life. Another part of her scanned each face, wondering if they could be involved in a conspiracy to hide her away here, taking away her name and her memories. Was old Miss Trant really as scatterbrained as she acted? Could Tony's red-faced grin be hiding something sinister behind it? The very thought seemed too absurd to contemplate.

Corrie hovered over her, even more protective than usual. Rachel came up to place an order for a turkey sandwich and a Reuben. Corrie assembled the sandwiches and put them in the toaster oven to warm up. Then she leaned against the counter and folded her arms, back to staring at Rachel. It was unnerving.

"What? Why are you looking at me like that?"

"I just want to make sure you're all right."

"Corrie, I'm *fine*. Really." Rachel cast about for something to distract her friend. "Here's something interesting. I can't find any stories about Michael online. Nothing about committing any crime. Doesn't that strike you as odd?"

Corrie's voice sharpened. "You shouldn't be looking at things online. That can't be good for your anxiety attacks. You want to decrease them, remember? The internet is filled with nothing but lies and negativity."

"Corrie. I'm not a child. Of course I can

look at things online." Honestly. Being protective was fine, but this was ridiculous. Corrie still frowned at her. "If he'd broken the law don't you think it would be documented somewhere?"

"There could be reasons for this man's crime being hushed up. I don't trust him, in any case. Why was he standing outside the Blue Whale watching you? I think he was up to no good."

"I suppose," Rachel said doubtfully.

When Tony came in for lunch, Rachel brought his usual sandwich over. She put the plate on the table and said, casually, "Tony, how did you find out about Michael stockpiling illegal guns?"

Tony frowned. Rachel's heart sank. "That newspaper clipping you showed me in the car, when you met me at the cabin."

Tony's expression cleared. "Oh, that. It was on my desk when I came in to work. After I traced your call back to that small town, I called the state police. They told me they'd received an anonymous tip that the man you were with, Sullivan, was involved with that isolationist group. They managed to locate the cabin. So I volunteered to see if I could catch you when he wasn't watching. But just before lunch, I heard that the state police let him go." Tony stopped speaking, and Rachel realized that he was angry and frustrated. "I suppose there *could* have been a mix-up," he said grudgingly. "But it doesn't change the fact that there was something suspicious about that man. He just *happened* to be around when you needed rescuing from some random strangers who grabbed you off the street?"

Rachel did not know what to think. Everyone she spoke to had a plausible explanation that painted Michael as a villain. All she had was an unreasoning voice deep inside that said he was on her side.

Either the rest of the world was crazy or she was.

She said, "So you don't know where the newspaper cutting came from?"

"No." Tony shrugged off his frustration. "Does it matter? There really are isolationists living up in the hills, and some of them do deal in illegal weapons. It's not an implausible scenario. It was enough to make me want to get you out of there right away."

Someone had used Tony to get her out of there on false pretenses.

Rachel felt a trickle of unease at the back of her mind. Somewhere, there was a puppet master pulling strings behind the scenes, manipulating people for his own reasons. But she was beginning to think the puppet master could not have been Tony. She admired Tony's dedication to his job, but he was not a mastermind. A good man, but not an especially subtle one. And whoever was behind this was both subtle and clever.

Talking to Corrie about her internet research had been a mistake. Corrie was a sweetheart, but she invariably passed on everything she heard. By this time, no doubt everyone in the café knew she'd been researching Michael online. If Rachel were going to figure out who was behind this, she'd have to be more circumspect. The last thing she needed was to make her friends more protective than they already were.

Tony hung around after lunch, lingering over his coffee. That trickle of unease came again, rising stronger. She had a feeling she knew what was coming. Sure enough, when she came to take his plate, Tony told Rachel, "You should go see Dr. Green."

Rachel forced herself to sound casual. "Not today, Tony. Maybe tomorrow."

Hovering nearby, Corrie clicked her tongue in reproof. "We'll see what the doctor has to say about that."

Rachel could feel her patience beginning to fray. "It doesn't matter what she says. Or what anyone else says. I have the right to decide what kind of treatment I receive."

Corrie only shook her head and went back to ring up a customer at the register.

After lunch, Corrie began her usual battle to shuffle Mrs. Benson and Miss Trant out. The old ladies sat close to each other at the counter, heads bent over their coffees, deep in discussion over the burning question of whether the new contestant on the latest reality show would be a success. Corrie flipped the sign on the door to read Closed.

"Ahem," Corrie said. She didn't even bother to pretend that she had actually been trying to clear her throat. "It's two o'clock, ladies."

"I just need to finish my coffee," Mrs. Benson said cheerfully.

"You go right ahead and clean up around us," Miss Trant added. "We won't mind."

Shaking her head, Corrie began to put the chairs up on the tables. Rachel started wiping down the counter. She had to fight the urge to hurry so she could leave sooner. *Act as if nothing is wrong.*

Corrie said, "Miss Trant, Mrs. Benson. Would you like me to put your coffee into to-go cups?"

"Oh, don't trouble yourself," Miss Trant said brightly. "I'm almost finished."

Rachel knew that both ladies relished their socializing, and ordinarily she didn't mind waiting a few minutes if it made their lives more pleasant. But today she could hardly restrain her impatience. As soon as Corrie walked her back to the apartment, Rachel was going to call Parker again. If he didn't have news of Michael, she'd figure out how to call Michael's boss herself. Someone, somewhere, knew where he was.

Finally, the two women drained their coffee cups. Swiftly, Rachel rinsed the cups out before they could change their minds. "I'll lock the door after you, ladies."

Corrie came in from the back room, carrying both their coats. "Not just yet."

Rachel looked at her. "Why not? Is there something more to do here?"

"Just one thing," Corrie said quietly.

The front door opened. "We're closed," Rachel called out automatically even as she turned to look. Then the words died in her throat.

Dr. Green herself stepped into the café. Corrie put down her coat on the counter. They both looked at Rachel. She felt trapped. "What?"

"I think you should come to my office for a therapy session." Dr. Green's eyes fixed Rachel in place, like a deer in the headlights of an oncoming truck.

"I don't want to take the medication any longer," Rachel said weakly.

"Even so," Corrie said. "You always told me how much the therapy sessions helped you. You've been through a dreadful experience, Rachel. You need help to get over it."

Rachel's eyes darted from one woman to the other, but she couldn't see how to escape without raising their suspicions even more. She had to play along, at least until she could find a way out. "All right. I'll just—I'll just stop off at home first." And try to call Michael again. Or Parker. The state police. Someone. She needed help.

She opened the back door. The doorway was blocked by the figure of Tony. He was smiling at her. But the kind pity in his eyes tightened the muscles in her stomach and raised the hairs along the back of her neck.

"I'm sorry, Rach. You can't leave. You've been under a lot of stress lately. The doc says you need to be kept calm. It's for the best."

Rachel whirled around and started for the front door. Dr. Green put a case on the table and pulled out a needle. "The medication doesn't have the same efficacy when injected, but it's easier to administer if a patient decides to be noncompliant."

Rachel backed up, shaking her head. "No. No more drugs. You're making me sicker, not better."

"I was afraid this might happen." Dr. Green filled the syringe with a clear liquid from a glass bottle. "Withdrawal can cause symptoms of paranoia. Trust me, you need this shot. Hold her," she said to Tony.

Tony nodded. His strong hands closed around Rachel's arms, holding her in place. "It'll be okay, Rach. We're going to take care of you."

"No drugs." Rachel tried to wrench herself free, but Tony's grip was too strong. "Please. I told you I don't want any more drugs."

"I'm afraid you're becoming overexcited," the doctor purred, her voice rich with satisfaction. Her smile was cruel, and the dark eyes that Rachel had always thought so warm now held nothing but malice, hard as stones. "This is for your own good."

"Let go of me!" Futile as it was, Rachel tried to wrench herself free. "This is wrong. You have no right to treat me like this. Stop this. Now."

Mrs. Benson clutched her knitting to her chest, mouth agape at all this drama. "Now, Rachel, dear, there's no need to get so upset. Sometimes you just have to take your medicine."

"Even if it's not pleasant." Miss Trant nodded. "Afterward, you'll be glad you did. The doctor knows best."

Rachel twisted around to face her boss. "Corrie, help me!"

Corrie blinked at her, her usual pleasant, absentminded countenance now looking completely baffled. "Rachel, I don't understand why you're making a fuss. You've always said that you trust Dr. Green. Just keep trusting her, and everything will be fine."

Rachel looked desperately around at the ring of kind, sympathetic, uncomprehending faces. This was like one of her nightmares, except this time she was awake. Though she knew it was futile, she couldn't help jerking back as the doctor's cold fingers touched her skin. Tony's grip tightened, holding her still.

A sharp prick as the needle pierced her arm, and darkness swallowed her whole.

When Rachel came to, she was lying in the

doctor's dim, restful therapy room. The pleasant scent of roses wafted in from the open window.

Rachel blinked, then sat up, looking around to orient herself. Why was she here? Dimly, she recalled struggling, arguing with Dr. Green. That made no sense. Dr. Green was only trying to help her. That strange man, Michael, had tried to make her doubt her own friends. How utterly ridiculous.

Dr. Green came into the room. "How are you feeling, dear?"

Rachel swung her legs off the therapy table. "I feel fine. What happened to me?" She rubbed her arm.

"You had a panic attack. Tony brought you to my office and I gave you a hypnosis session. Then you took a nap." The doctor held out a small white pill and a glass of water. "You need to take this now."

Rachel hesitated. Dr. Green had an odd look in her eyes. Intent, almost cold. It made Rachel uneasy.

Oh, she was imagining things. Rachel took the pill and swallowed it obediently. Then a wave of nausea washed over her and she had to rush for the old-fashioned bathroom that had been part of the old cottage when it was first built.

Afterward, Rachel splashed cold water on her face and patted it dry with a hand towel that hung on a hook. She raised the narrow window and put her head out. The window looked onto a side alley, a pleasant place with bright red geraniums planted in enormous terra-cotta pots. It was quiet, and the spicy scent of the geraniums mixed with the air fresh off the sea was refreshing. Rachel closed her eyes and took a few moments to breathe in the cool, clean air. The sick feeling passed.

"I'm sorry," she said, when she came out. "I've never had that reaction before."

Dr. Green ran her eyes up and down Rachel's body, assessing her. "It's understandable. You're still feeling stressed from your traumatic experiences. You need more rest. You can take the medication later, when you're more relaxed."

Rachel reached for her purse, which always hung on the hook on the back of the door. "Oh. I must have left my purse back at the Blue Whale. Can I pay you later?"

Dr. Green waved a hand. "That will be fine, dear."

For some reason, Rachel could still smell

the spicy scent of the geraniums, even though the door to the bathroom was closed. No, it wasn't quite the same smell. This was something woodsy, with a subtle hint of spice to it... A memory tugged at the back of her mind, and she frowned in an effort to recall it.

She felt oddly uneasy. It was as though that man, Michael, were there with her. Why did she connect this scent with him? Then the memory speared through the mists of uncertainty like a sunbeam straight from Heaven. As if she stood on solid ground again.

Michael was here in the cottage. Her heart thudded, terror and eagerness coursed through her veins. She was terrified. She was elated. She could not sort out *what* she was feeling. All she knew was that she had to act as if nothing was amiss. If Michael were discovered here, no one would believe he wasn't stalking her. He'd probably end up in jail. She composed her face into tranquility.

It was broad daylight when they had finally released Michael. On his way out, the quiet man gave him his card. "Let me know if you find out anything about Dr. Vance. I have looked into his financials for another case. There are some very shifty things going on with the money at that company. I haven't been able to prove anything, but I have a hunch something is wrong there. If you need help, let me know."

Michael tucked the card in his pocket. "If I find anything, I'll give you a call."

Michael had begun dialing Rachel's number even before he started the car. No answer. Perhaps she was at work and couldn't pick up, but a sick uncertainty turned in the pit of his stomach.

Once he crossed the city limits of Sleepy Cove, he slowed his pace, scanning the sidewalk. The Blue Whale Café was closed and dark. The curtains drawn at Rachel's apartment. On a hunch, Michael headed toward Dr. Green's clinic.

Off to one side of the house was a side door to the alley. After a quick look up and down the alley, he tried the door. It opened noiselessly, and he slipped inside. A dark hallway ran the length of the house. From a room off to the left, Michael heard voices.

With infinite care, he cracked the door open and peered in. Rachel stood there, facing a woman with her hair pulled back into a tight bun. She looked like the stereotype of a scientist. It seemed almost redundant that she was wearing a white lab coat.

She struck Michael as an actor playing a part. The doctor was saying, "I hope you weren't too badly upset by that man and the things he said to you. I know that that type of person can be very convincing. And they are invariably quite charming when they try to convince their victims to go along with them. But you cannot trust that sort of person. They will say anything to get you to do what they want."

Michael clenched his fists. There was nothing he could do to stop this woman from pouring poison into Rachel's ear.

"What are you looking for, dear?"

"My phone." Rachel patted her pockets again. "Dr. Green, have you seen my phone? I can't seem to find it anywhere."

"Don't you remember, dear?" The doctor smiled at her. Even from a room away, Michael could see that the warmth did not reach her eyes. "You gave up your phone months ago. Said it made you anxious to have it around. I think you were not feeling up to the responsibility of having to deal with the outside world. All part of your anxiety. Perfectly normal. Perhaps in a couple months, we might consider getting you a new phone. It's better for you to stick to a simple life at the moment. The internet is far too negative for you in your fragile state just now."

Rachel's brow wrinkled. "No, that can't be right. I had a phone. I remember—" Her voice broke off.

The doctor said, "But it's so hard to be sure about these things, isn't it? I know you have been through a great deal of stress lately. I think it might be affecting your mind. Sadly, one issue with the medication that you are on is the possibility of a loss of memory."

"I know I had a phone," Rachel said obstinately. "I remember it clearly."

The doctor shook her head, still smiling. "I think you might want to consider the possibility that man and the stress of having to deal with him has influenced you. It was awful what he did to you. I know that you were upset by it, though you're trying to put up a bold front. I just want to say that I hope you didn't take him seriously when he acted as if you were someone important to him. You must have realized that he was only projecting his needs onto you. The poor man."

"I did tell him he should go see you," Rachel said, the words dragged from her slowly, as if against her will. "I told him that you could help him."

"I only wish I had had the chance," the doctor said with every appearance of sincerity.

Rachel frowned, but she did not say anything more. The doctor had worn her down. No wonder confident Nora had been transformed into timid Rachel, if this was what she'd had to face every day.

The doctor gestured toward the couch. "You should lie down. You need to rest. You are very tired."

Slowly, Rachel moved toward the couch. "I do feel tired. You're right about that. And I think I will go lie down."

The doctor patted her on her shoulder. "Don't worry about anything, dear. After you've had a nice rest, you can take your pill. That's what you need right now. I will take care of you. You trust me, don't you?"

"Yes, of course I do." Rachel nodded. Michael wanted to hit something.

Rachel took a deep breath. "But those pills are making me sick. I don't want to take them anymore." She paused, clearly steeling herself. "I don't want to, and I am not going to. That's final."

Dr. Green shook her head slowly. "I was

afraid it might come to this. Your time with that man has confused you so much you don't know who to trust." She sighed. "But, Rachel, I will make sure you get the help you need. There's a facility outside of Eugene where they can help you. You need more supervision, to ensure you take the medication on a timely basis."

Rachel stiffened. "You mean a hospital. No. I don't want that. I have the right to refuse any treatment that I don't want."

"Actually, dear, that's not correct." Dr. Green was smiling. Clearly, she was loving this moment. "In my office, I have a copy of a piece of paper, signed by you, giving me power of attorney."

"No," was all Rachel said, but the fear in her voice wrenched at Michael's heart. He could see she believed the doctor.

Dr. Green's smile deepened. "You might not remember this, but some months ago, when we first started your therapy, you were afraid that you might not be able to guide your own decisions at some point. So you signed over to me a medical power of attorney, authorizing me to guide your medical decisions. I can show you the paper if you don't believe me. I don't want to do this, but if I have to, I will go to the authorities and have you declared mentally unfit to make your own decisions. That paper gives me the authority to direct your medical future. What you need right now is isolation and rest. Supervised medical treatment. It was a good try for you to function in the outside world—get a job and be self-sufficient—but clearly that's not the case any longer. If you resist, I will have no choice but to take matters into my own hands. I will see that you get the care that you need."

Rachel's voice rose. "Against my will? You're going to have me locked up and you're going to decide what's done with me? That can't be right. There has to be something I can do to change that. I have rights."

"You signed over those rights to me, dear." The doctor had Rachel just where she wanted her. "I'll make the call now, tell them to send someone to pick you up. You just wait here. At least I know you're not going to leave town on your own."

"I understand," Rachel whispered. The doctor turned to leave. Quickly, Michael ducked into the bathroom across the hall and swung the door closed. He listened to the doctor's footsteps moving away. Down the hall, a door shut. Michael slipped across the hall to the room that held Rachel. Rachel stood in the center of the room, her eyes closed and her lips moving. He thought perhaps she was praying.

Before she could move or do anything else, Michael was behind her. He covered her mouth with his hand. He whispered in her ear, "Don't scream."

NINE

Rachel turned around. Her eyes were dark, the pupils dilated wide, but she did not make a sound. Michael lifted his hand from her mouth. He had been afraid she would try to scream or run away. He had expected some sign of fear.

The last thing he had anticipated was for her to slide her arms around his neck and hug him tightly, as if afraid he might disappear.

Without conscious thought, Michael's arms came around her waist and he pulled her to him. He had been so afraid he'd never be this close to her again. His arms tightened around her.

After a moment, Rachel stiffened, as if a thought had just struck her. She pulled away. Michael pushed a strand of hair from her face. "Are you all right?"

"I didn't mean to do that," Rachel said, her voice shaky. Her hands still rested on his chest.

As if suddenly realizing this, she stepped back. "You weren't answering your phone. I thought something must have happened to you."

"Please don't apologize." He meant it, with all his heart. She was here. With him. Happiness flooded through him, almost a dizzying reaction after his sleepless night and hours of worry. All Michael wanted was to be left alone with Rachel and for the world to retreat. But he had to concentrate on saving her life first. "How are you feeling?"

Rachel clasped her hands together, gripping them tightly. "I don't know what to believe anymore. My whole world has been turned upside down." She looked down and spoke to her hands, very softly. "You feel like the only real thing in my world right now."

"When I heard that doctor talking to you— for a moment, I thought you were buying the lies she was spinning."

"I wanted to." Rachel's voice was so low Michael barely caught the words. "That's what is so strange. Even though what she was telling me went against everything I knew was true, I still *wanted* to believe her."

Michael itched to pull her back toward him, circle his arms around her and never let her go. He did not dare. "We don't have time to talk now. My car is waiting at the end of the alley. We can be gone before Dr. Green finishes her call. They won't be expecting you to leave town."

"I don't see how I can get away. They've taken my purse and my phone. I can't see him from here, but I'm sure Tony is watching the entrance to the alley."

"I can get you out the way I came in. We can be halfway to Eugene before they know you're gone."

In the half-light, Michael could not read the expression on her face clearly, but the way her shoulders hunched forward told its own tale of loss and confusion. "I don't even know who *they* are. That's the worst of it. I'm doubting everyone I thought was my friend. People I would trust with my life two weeks ago—now I question everything they say. I don't know who to trust."

It made his heart ache to see her looking so lost. Daringly, he reached out, touched her cheek lightly. Her skin was so cold. He turned her to face him. "Trust in God. And you know that I'm on your side, no matter what."

"Are you?" Finally, she looked up and her eyes met his. "Why did you never tell me you were engaged to Nora?"

Michael let his hand drop. "I was going to tell you, but the timing never seemed right. First, you thought I was a mad stalker, then you were kidnapped. When you finally started to listen to me, I didn't want you to feel pressured. I thought it would be better for you to remember yourself first before you remembered us, what we had."

"Not knowing made me feel worse," Rachel said. "This changes things."

"It changes nothing. Not to me."

"You want me to wear Nora's clothes. To step into her shoes—literally and romantically, as far as your relationship is concerned. All I have to do is agree to let Dr. Parker repair Nora's memories and you and she can pick up where you left off."

Michael struggled to find the right words to make his feelings clear. "I won't deny I want you to have your life back. You've been cut off from your past, you have no future here. You've just been drifting, in limbo. I want you to be whole and healed, the complete woman you were before."

She studied his face. Michael wasn't sure what his expression showed: resignation, rejection, hurt. Whether she realized it or not, Rachel was pushing him away. Maybe that embrace when she first saw him had just been an emotional reaction to finding someone she could rely on. She wasn't looking for a lasting relationship with him.

If that was what she wanted, he would accept it. Set the pain aside. Deal with it later. He said, "I will help you get out of here. We have to go now. Are you willing to trust me?"

"Yes," Rachel said slowly. "But, Michael… I don't want to simply escape. To sneak away in the night."

The sudden lift of her chin and the crusading light in her eye—the familiar gestures and expression were so like the old Nora that it hurt. But he couldn't let her take the risk. "If you stay, they'll lock you up. We have to go. Now."

"No." She shook her head. "You misunderstand me. I mean I don't want to let them get away with this." Outrage strengthened her voice. "These people robbed me, taking everything away from me, even my own identity. I don't want to just run away. I want to stop them from ever doing this to someone else. I need to get proof."

Michael said, "The best proof would be you, yourself."

"You mean Nora, not me. I don't have her

memories. I may have some of the skills that she had, but I'm no genius medical researcher."

"If you go to the authorities, you can prove that you really are Nora Stewart. Fingerprints, DNA. Nora Stewart, missing for months, reappears after having been brainwashed—"

"How do I prove amnesia? People could just say I'd run away on my own. No one would convict Dr. Green based on my word."

Michael could not deny it. That had been his first reaction after all, when Parker had described the condition to him.

"Corrie, Tony, half the town knows I've been struggling with anxiety issues. This would sound as if I've added paranoia to the lineup. No, I need something tangible. The best place to look is Dr. Green's office."

"I don't like it," Michael said. "It's too risky. If they catch you, they'll start in with those mind games and get you twisted around in your thinking again. The safest course of action is to get you away from this place while they think you're still cooperating. First, let me get you away from here. Then I'll come back and look around."

"But that will be too late! Once I leave, whoever is behind this will know that the game is up. They'll cover their tracks. They will probably disappear and move to another town. I don't want to waste this opportunity. This is the only chance that I have to find out what is going on."

She peered out the window again. "I just want to go through the doctor's office. She must be the one behind this. She controls the supply of drugs, and I think those drugs are what have been making me feel so funny. She's very good at manipulating people. She made Tony and Corrie feel guilty about not taking care of me. And I don't want them to be held responsible if she's arrested. I want to find proof that she is the guilty one."

"Do you think she would have that information in her office?"

"It's a very small office. She doesn't employ anyone as an assistant. So far as I know, she doesn't have many patients." Rachel paused, looking thoughtful. "Actually, I've never seen another patient in her office. Strange, it never occurred to me to wonder about that. But I don't know that she's ever seen anyone else in town."

"A one-patient doctor."

"I'm certain that she's kept some records. She's too much of a scientist not to take notes and track my progress. If Dr. Vance is behind this, he'd want daily reports. This is his wonder drug, and he'd want to know everything about what happens here."

Michael said suddenly, "Was that a memory? Are you starting to remember Dr. Vance?"

Rachel stopped to consider this. "I'm—I'm not sure how I know that about him. I just do. Well, it makes sense that he'd be like that, doesn't it? Those supersmart people want to micromanage their businesses. This whole setup could be just him and Dr. Green." Her tone brightened. "I don't know if there needs to be that many other people involved in this town. She's very good at manipulating people."

"*If* she is arrested. Don't get ahead of yourself. You still need to find some proof."

"All I need is to get her out of the office long enough for me to go through it. And see if I can find anything. Will you help me?"

"Of course I will." Michael gave in to the impulse to reach out and take hold of her arms. He did not pull her toward him. Not yet. "You know I'll always be there for you. I love you."

"Would you still love me if I didn't regain my memories of being Nora?" Her expression was focused, intent. "I need to know where I stand, as I am now. I don't want to stop being Rachel. Even if you are in love with Nora."

He started to speak and she held up a hand to stop him. "Listen to me. We don't have much time. I want your help—I need it. But if you're helping me because you think Nora is going to come back to you…don't. I don't *want* to be this Nora woman. Being Rachel is *all I've ever known*. Losing myself…it's like facing death. I can't just willingly give that up to go back to being someone else. No matter how important Nora is to you."

Michael waited for her to finish. "To me, you're still the same woman. Different face, different hair, but none of that comes near the essential qualities that I love you for. I don't distinguish between the way you acted before and the way you act now. You're still the same person. There's no difference, not to me."

Rachel could not remember a time when she had felt so cold before. Frozen, as she had been after he had kissed her in the cabin. She whispered, "To me, there's all the difference in the world."

Michael's hands dropped. It was difficult to be sure in this dim half-light, but she thought his expression had changed to that impassive facade he always adopted whenever he was feeling uncertain or upset. "Okay, then. I'll call the doctor, distract her to give you a few minutes to search. If you can't find anything in that time, then it's too well hidden and we'll need a warrant to do a proper search."

Michael moved to the door, listened intently. "I can still hear her on the phone." He hesitated, turned back. "Rachel—be careful." Then he was gone.

Rachel stood there, heart beating very fast. It was the first time he'd ever called her by her name, instead of Nora. She would have expected to feel happy about it. Instead, she felt an indescribable sense of loss. A door had closed between them. And what should have felt like victory tasted bitter as ashes in her mouth.

Dr. Green came back into the room. She looked different, smaller somehow, dressed in a dark sweater and jeans, ordinary. It took Rachel a moment to realize she wasn't wearing her white lab coat. As if she'd been playing a role and no longer needed the coat as a prop.

Dr. Green raised her eyebrows. "Rachel. You're not lying down."

Rachel clasped her hands together. "I wanted to apologize," she stammered. She hunched her shoulders forward and cast her gaze humbly down toward the doctor's feet. "I shouldn't have argued with you earlier. I was rude—especially after all the things you've done for me."

"Well, you were rather impertinent, dear." No human being should ever sound that smug. It was nauseating. "But I'm surprised to hear you admit it. After your little tantrum this afternoon, I mean. You were so hysterical."

Rachel opened her mouth to argue, then stopped. A swift glance upward was all she needed. That satisfied gleam in Dr. Green's eyes meant that the woman was goading her, driving her to get upset. She remembered Michael saying that Dr. Green had been let go from her previous job amidst claims that she had been cruel to the patients under her care.

"You might be right," Rachel admitted. "I know you only want what is best for me. I can't seem to relax. The thought of going back to a hospital is, well, it's terrifying. Your therapy sessions always make me feel better. Do you think we could have another session?"

"Of course, my dear." Dr. Green's smile widened. "I thought you'd come to see things my way sooner or later. Let me guess. You finally took one of those little white pills that I gave you, didn't you?"

"Oh, you were so right about those pills," Rachel said earnestly. "I knew taking one of them would make me see things differently. You were right, as you always are. I don't know why I didn't listen to you in the first place."

Rachel was afraid she might be piling it on too thick, but the doctor only smirked. "You poor thing. That nasty man got you so confused that you didn't know who your friends were. I'm so glad you came to your senses."

Michael had better come through with his promised distraction soon. Therapy was the only excuse that Rachel could come up with that she was sure the doctor would be willing to listen to. But if Michael didn't hurry, she might find herself floating in a happy fog of delusions.

Just then, the office phone rang. Dr. Green blinked, looking very surprised. "What on earth?" Then she relaxed. "It's probably just a salesman. Nothing important, in any case. I will let it go to voice mail."

"You should answer it." Rachel was counting on the doctor wanting to maintain the illusion that she was a bona fide medical professional who was dedicated to running a successful business. "It might be someone with a medical emergency. After all, it's not as if I'm your only patient, right?"

Dr. Green hesitated. Then she nodded reluctantly. "That's a good point, dear. I'll just take care of the person on the phone and be right with you." She turned to the front hall, where the receptionist's desk was, with its telephone and printer and all the other stage props designed to make this place look like an ordinary doctor's office. Rachel had never even questioned why Dr. Green didn't have a receptionist. Corrie was right; she *had* been too trusting. It was past time to change that.

Quietly, Rachel waited until she heard Dr. Green pick up the phone. Then she closed the door to the therapy room and just as quietly went to the door to Dr. Green's office.

Even in the office, she could clearly hear the doctor on the phone. Rachel searched quickly through the room. Bookcases, file cabinets, desk drawers, everything was unlocked and innocent. Rachel could find nothing that looked like medical records. Surely Dr. Green would keep them here, in the office? The cottage didn't have that many rooms, after all.

In the front hall, Dr. Green's voice rose. "What do you mean, allegations against me? I can't believe you're bringing up that old business in Salem. I was cleared of all wrongdoing. You can't take away my license based on innuendo and false allegations. It's totally unethical."

From the sound of things, Michael was pretending to be some kind of medical board investigator. Certainly, he was keeping the doctor's mind fully focused on their conversation for the moment, but Rachel knew she was running out of time. She ran her hands down the insides of the desk drawers, looking for any secret compartments. Everything was depressingly open and straightforward. Rachel turned around in a circle.

The doctor's lab coat was hanging on a hook on the door. In one of the side pockets, Rachel saw the doctor's little voice recorder. She hesitated, head cocked, while she listened to the furious conversation coming from the front hall. Then she darted over and took the voice recorder out of the pocket. Swiftly, she retreated back into the therapy room and closed the door behind her.

Making sure the volume was set to low, Rachel pressed Play and held the speaker to her ear. She heard Dr. Green's voice, smooth and professional with its deep soothing tones. As Rachel listened, it felt to her as if the sky were falling.

Snatches of phrases leaped out at her, but she could not take it all in. It was too horrible.

Your name is Rachel Ann Garrett.

You love living in Sleepy Cove.

You cannot leave Sleepy Cove.

Something terrible will happen if you go past the city limits...

Dr. Green is the only doctor you have faith in. You always want to do what she tells you...

You trust Tony and Corrie completely. They are your friends. They only want what is best for you...

You grew up on a small farm near the Wallowa Mountains. When the farmhouse burned down, you lost both your parents...

TEN

The show was over. She had seen behind the curtain and knew it for an illusion. There was no safety here.

The doctor's office. The café. All her neighbors in Sleepy Cove. People she counted as friends. People she trusted. Everything around her was familiar, dearly loved, safe.

Everything was a lie.

Rachel had accepted on an intellectual level that she was being lied to. But the reality of listening to Dr. Green's betrayal was like opening the door of her own house and finding it filled with filth and corruption. A cold weight settled like concrete in the pit of her stomach. She felt sick to the core of her soul.

Finally, Rachel lowered the voice recorder and looked around her. It felt as if eons had passed since she found out what really was going on. In reality, it had probably only been a few moments. There wasn't time for further delay.

Rachel darted across the room to the door to the hall. She put her hand on the doorknob, then she hesitated. The doctor was still talking in the reception area by the front door. Treading quietly, Rachel went to the side door that led to the bathroom and tried the window that led to the alley. The window was wide enough for her to thrust her head out of it, but it was too narrow for her shoulders. She could probably wriggle through eventually, but it would be noisy and painful and take far too much time.

She stuffed the recorder into her pocket and looked around. Michael couldn't hold Dr. Green's attention for very much longer. Carefully, Rachel eased open the office window. Clearly, it had not been opened in some time. As she lifted the sash, it squeaked in protest.

Rachel froze, holding her breath. Dr. Green's voice did not pause. If anything, her voice had raised. She was reaching new heights of invective, describing what she thought of Michael's allegations. Rachel tried again, raising the window sash slowly until there was enough room for her to wriggle through.

The alley was empty. Michael was nowhere in sight. His SUV idled at the end of the alley, just where he had said it would be, but as she moved toward it, a white van drove past and stopped, blocking the way out. Rachel dropped behind one of the large terra-cotta pots. After a minute, she cautiously peeked over the top. The alley was clear.

She dashed down to Michael's car. The door was locked and no one was inside. A glance up and down the street showed no sign of Michael.

Cautiously, she made her way along the side of the house and peered around the front. Then immediately she ducked out of sight, pressing against the wall as though she could merge with it. She'd only had one quick glance, but she had seen enough. Michael, head hanging down as though he had been knocked out, feet dragging as the two kidnappers hauled him down the walkway toward a waiting white van.

Something had gone very wrong. The only thing she was certain of was that she could not remain where she was. Dr. Green would find her if she didn't leave in a hurry.

There must be a pay phone in town somewhere, but for the moment she couldn't think where. And she couldn't borrow a phone from anyone without questions she could not answer and explanations she did not want to make.

Michael. She had to stay free so she could rescue him. She had to get away, get to someone who could help her. She couldn't do it on her own.

It felt like betrayal to walk away, knowing he was in trouble, but she couldn't think of what else to do.

Once outside the town, she would hitchhike to the nearest big town and find a phone. Look up the phone number for Michael's friend, that doctor. He knew Michael's boss. He could convince him to help find Michael.

Her mind made up, Rachel sprinted down the block. She had to get out of sight of Dr. Green's cottage. It felt as if she had a target painted on her back. As she turned the corner onto Main Street, however, she slowed down, forced herself to keep to a relaxed pace, act as if nothing were wrong. It was maddening to go so slow while her heart thudded as if running a race. But above all, she could not afford to raise suspicion.

The fog was swirling in from the ocean now, thin gray tendrils reaching out like greedy fingers to grasp at the Victorian gingerbread cutouts on the houses, wrapping around them, blurring the lines between the familiar and the unknown in a wash of gray. Behind crept a thicker wall of mist that flowed like a slowly moving fortress inexorably toward her.

Rachel took a breath, trying to summon up courage she did not feel. Then she plunged into the fog and everything changed. Visibility was reduced to only a foot or two in front of her. The dim lighting threw shadows across the faces of people she'd seen every day for months now, warping innocent, friendly faces into something sinister.

Rachel wished there had been time to listen to the whole audiotape. She had pressed Stop in midsentence, too upset to hear the rest of the doctor's lies. But that meant she had no idea who else might be involved in this web of deceit. She forced herself to saunter down the street—and scanned each face as she passed. Anyone could betray her.

As if on cue, a hand landed on her shoulder and Rachel almost jumped out of her skin. She turned around. "Oh! Mrs. Gibbs. You startled me."

Her voice sounded about two octaves higher than normal, but the other woman didn't seem to notice anything odd. "I'm so sorry, dear." Mrs. Gibbs smiled at her. She was staring at Rachel intently. "What are you doing out on your own like this? I thought Tony was walking out with you."

Rachel forced a laugh. It sounded more like a wheeze to her. "Mrs. Gibbs, you make it sound like he's courting me, or something old-fashioned like that. He's just a friend, nothing more." *Act natural. As if you weren't on the run for your life.* The moment Mrs. Gibbs, or any of the other townspeople, thought that something was wrong, they would notify Tony or Dr. Green.

"Well, maybe I should go with you, make sure you don't have one of your attacks. Helena Trant was saying that you had a nervous breakdown right in the middle of the café today, and Dr. Green had to sedate you on the spot! I'm sorry I wasn't there," Mrs. Gibbs concluded, with evident regret. "But I can go with you now."

Rachel wasn't sure whether the woman was acting out of misplaced loyalty or because she didn't want to miss out on a front-row seat in case Rachel broke down in hysterics in the middle of Main Street, but in either case she could not afford any more delay. Firmly, she said, "Mrs. Gibbs, I don't need an escort."

"But what would the doctor say if I let you walk by yourself? Honestly, Rachel, dear—"

"But that's just it," Rachel broke in. "This is part of my new therapy routine. I have to walk by myself for a whole mile every day. The doctor said it would be very good for my health."

Thankfully, Mrs. Gibbs didn't think to ask *which* doctor Rachel was referring to. Dr. Parker probably would agree with her that it would be good if she got far away from this town.

"Well, I guess I'll see you at the café tomorrow, as usual."

Not if I have anything to say about it. Rachel gave Mrs. Gibbs a farewell nod, which hopefully might be taken for agreement, and strode briskly down the sidewalk before the other woman could make any further remarks. She rounded the corner and broke into a steady jog.

Now the clock was ticking. If Dr. Green or Tony were out hunting for her—and Rachel had no doubt they were—then Rachel had to make it out of town before one of them came across Mrs. Gibbs, or they'd know in which direction she was headed.

Once outside the city limits, the pressure would be off. That was the last place they'd think to look for her. Ironically, in creating these barriers in her mind, Dr. Green had provided Rachel with the means of escape.

Of course, she still had to find a way to make it past the city limits, without anyone kidnapping her or giving her drugs. Just herself, Rachel, on her own.

She'd deal with that when she got there. Rachel turned onto a side street that provided a shortcut to the main highway. The fog was thinner here. The street was deserted. With no one around to notice, she lengthened her stride until she was running—literally running for her life.

It was all she could think to do. It was enough. She still had to make it past the city limits.

The gray mist grew denser as she approached the main highway, condensing into moisture that soaked into her hair and trickled cold rivulets of water down her neck. Rachel dropped back down to a slow jog. She was panting now and pressed her hand against her ribs to stop the burning stitch in her side.

A car whizzed past her, heading out of town. For a moment, Rachel was tempted to flag it down, but she dismissed the notion. Inside the city limits, it was too risky. Nine out of ten tourists would pull over if Tony flagged them down. And she'd be better off traveling on foot than dealing with the tenth. No, if she was going to try to hitchhike, it had to wait until she was out of town.

The time dragged endlessly, at least it felt like it did. In reality, probably only ten minutes or so passed before the sign loomed out of the dark. *You're Leaving Sleepy Cove! Come Again Soon!*

The city limits.

Rachel put her hand on the signpost. It wasn't just the exertion that made her breath come quickly now. The metal post was cold, and wet from the dew, but she gripped it tightly. The old familiar roiling began in her stomach. In a moment, she would start to feel like she had to throw up.

It was no good telling herself that her reaction was caused by drugs and external conditioning, that she had been brainwashed by evil people manipulating her for their own ends. That didn't change the visceral reaction. The fear was all too real.

Rachel could not afford to stand here and think about that. She had to do this, or Michael would not survive. She only wished there were someone with her, that she didn't have to face this alone.

No.

There in the darkness, surrounded by doubt and fear, Rachel realized the truth.

She was not alone.

There was One who would always be with her in the dark places of her life, and He was with her now. Lost as she was in this swirling fog of uncertainty, her faith in God was the only anchor she could cling to. *Lord, You are with me even when I am lost in the dark places of my mind. I am not alone because You are here now. You walk beside me even here.*

Rachel had always prayed that the Lord would walk with her on her daily journey. Never before had she realized how literal the prayer had been. She whispered, "My grace is sufficient for thee: for my strength is made perfect in weakness."

She had never felt so weak in her life.

Rachel took a deep breath. She focused her attention on the nearest line of bushes. It was probably no more than a thousand feet away, but it might as well have been a thousand miles. She could never make it that far.

Nausea gripped her stomach. She fought the urge to throw up.

One step. She could do that.

She shut her eyes and concentrated on nothing but moving her right foot one step ahead of her body. *Just one step.*

Then she stepped past the sign.

Don't hesitate. Don't think. Just take one more step.

One more step.

Then another. And another.

She was doing it. She couldn't walk all the way to Portland, but she could take one step more. That was all she had to do. Take that one step. And know she was not alone.

Rachel counted her steps. One, two, three, four, five. She stopped and opened her eyes. She was standing on the side of the highway. Ahead of her was nothing but the road, bordered by hills on one side and the crashing surf on the other.

She had done it. She had left Sleepy Cove. Rachel did not stop to look back. If she turned her head, she'd see the small town that held every friend she could ever remember.

Rachel started walking. Every nerve ending prickled with awareness of how exposed and vulnerable she was so close to town.

There was a bend in the road ahead. Once past that, she would be out of sight of the town. And it would be fully dark soon. That would make it harder to hitchhike, but it would also provide protection from anyone who might be looking for her.

She kept walking. The steady drizzle started to soak through her jacket, and her feet were growing cold. At least while she walked the movement would keep her warm.

Rachel didn't know how long she walked. It felt like forever. It was probably closer to an hour before she came to the next sign of civilization. A gas station and a mini-mart, both closed at this time of night. She tried the pay phone next to the gas station, but it was out of order.

Now what?

Rachel stood there in the dark, feeling desperate. She was exhausted, cold and out of options. She had no idea how long it would take her to get to the next town. Her feet were turning to ice.

After about ten minutes, a car drove past and pulled over to the side of the road ahead of her. Rachel approached it warily. It was a sleek foreign model that Rachel did not recognize. The passenger window rolled down.

Peering in, Rachel could see by the dashboard light a woman peering back out at her. Rachel couldn't make out many details, but she had an impression of dark hair and a pale face with bright lipstick. A smooth, confident voice inquired, "Need a lift?"

The rising wind lashed raindrops down the full length of her body. This could well be a trap, but by this point Rachel had to take the chance. She made up her mind. "Yes, please."

The passenger door unlocked with a click and Rachel slid gratefully into the car's warmth. In the light from the dashboard, she got the impression of a woman in a business suit, her hair pulled up into a French twist, as sleekly sophisticated as the car itself. Rachel ran her hand over the smooth leather of the seat. "I'm afraid I'm going to make your car damp."

The woman shrugged this off. "It's the company's car, not mine." Her voice was sharp, the words clipped, but she did not sound unfriendly as she added, "Where are you headed for? I'm going as far as Eugene."

"Could you let me off at the nearest town?" Rachel racked her brain to think where the next town was. She had no memory of ever going there. South of Sleepy Cove, the coastline mostly consisted of rocky cliffs and isolated beaches. No towns large enough to have stores that would be open at night.

"Well, I don't mind the company." The

woman put the car in gear. "Being a sales rep means a lot of driving, especially since my area covers the coast and the Willamette Valley. Having someone to talk to while I drive makes for a nice change."

Rachel cocked her head. "Have we met? Your voice sounds familiar." A memory tantalized her, hovering just out of reach.

"You meet a lot of people in my line of work," the woman said. "Have you ever attended a medical convention in Portland? I meet a lot of people there."

"Possibly," Rachel said cautiously. At least, she had the idea that Nora had gone to a lot of those.

"Were you at the convention last year where the sales rep—not one of ours, I'm glad to say—tried to get too friendly with one of the waitresses? She took offense to something he said and a carafe of wine ended up all over his, er, brochures."

The incident sounded vaguely familiar to Rachel. Yes, she *had* been at that convention. That explained why the woman's voice sounded familiar, at least.

"So, what are you doing out on the coast?"

"My car broke down—I was in an accident." Or so she had been told.

"That can happen." The woman was sympathetic. "Easy enough to get into an accident on these twisty narrow roads, all slick from the rain."

Rachel noticed that the winding road didn't seem to bother the woman at all. Indeed, she steered around the curves at a high speed, handling the car with cool confidence. Rachel continued improvising a story. "My friend said he was going to give me a lift, but—well, he wasn't there when I got to the place we were supposed to meet."

"He stood you up?" The woman shook her head. "Men. Sometimes, I don't know why we put up with them."

"It *was* terrible," Rachel agreed. "I just wanted to get away from all the unpleasantness and go somewhere that didn't hold any bad memories."

The woman accepted this story, which, thin as it was, at least had the merit of being the truth. "I can drop you off, but there aren't any more towns for a good long while. I've got to call on a client in Eugene. That's probably the closest town, but it will be an hour or so before we get there."

Rachel racked her brain. Dr. Parker was probably one of the few people who would believe her story. He knew Michael's boss from their time in the army. The boss would listen to him, get people out looking for Michael. After the interrogation at the police station about the kidnapping, the state police might think Rachel was fantasizing or something. Especially if she had to accuse Tony on the basis of a tape recording.

"Could I borrow your cell phone?"

The woman shook her head. "No cell reception out here in these hills. It's too isolated."

Rachel peered out the window. They had turned off the coast highway. The car was rushing up a hill. Trees blurred past her window. She tried to remember where that small town had been that Michael had taken her, but she could not even begin to think where that might be.

She had to get help for Michael. Anything could be happening to him right now. He might be dead. Bile rose in her throat, leaving a bitter taste, and she closed her eyes for a moment as though that could fend off the images of Michael injured, in pain…gone from this life altogether.

She had forgotten how much being in love could hurt. It opened you up to joy but also to the possibility of loss. Every time Michael

went off on a mission, she had faced the possibility that he might not come back.

The memory slipped into her mind as if it
had always been there. Perhaps it had. Was
she starting to remember Nora's life now? She
could still remember every detail of her life
back in Sleepy Cove. She sighed and slumped
back against the seat.

"Tired? I know how that feels. This client is
going to be my last call for the day."

"Isn't it late to be making a business call?"
Rachel ventured.

"Yes, unfortunately. This guy's a night owl,
does most of his work at night. Sometimes it
feels as if I'm spending all my time trying to
please arrogant self-entitled businessmen who
think the whole world revolves around their
whims." The woman snorted. "One of these
days, I'm going to get enough money to tell all
of them what they can do with their annoying
little habits…"

The woman went on, telling Rachel some
lengthy, involved story about trying to please
a client long enough to get them to place an
order. Rachel didn't need to ask questions. The
woman seemed glad of a chance for a sympathetic listener. It was restful not to have to do
anything but sit for a while.

At least they were well into the Coast Range now. Snow was piled up on the side of the road, but the highway was clear as the car reached the pass and began to wind down into the Willamette Valley. It wouldn't be long now before they reached Eugene.

Rachel should have felt excited, but she'd been running on terror and adrenaline for too many hours now. Fatigue had seeped into her bones. She ached with weariness. There was nothing more she could do right now. She could close her eyes. Just for a moment.

Rachel didn't think she dozed, but she was jolted to full awareness by the car slowing. "Are we there yet?"

"Almost," the woman said.

She blinked and looked out the window. They passed through metal gates that clashed shut behind them. A small, squat building lay ahead, long wings stretching out on either side. It looked like an office building, except for the lack of windows. Fear jolted through Rachel, and she sat upright. "I don't like it here. I don't want to stay."

The woman peered at her. "Why? Have you been here before?"

"Yes." Rachel spoke without thinking, and that frightened her more. Where had that certainty come from? "No. Maybe. I don't know why, but this place looks familiar and I don't like it. I want to leave. Now."

"Ah," the woman said softly. "I wondered if you were starting to remember."

Terror battered her. This was bad. This was very bad. A security guard was heading toward the car, and Rachel knew he was not going to help her.

"Don't fight," the woman said. "If you try to run, Smithy'll just bring you back." Her lips curved up into a smile. "And there are ways to hurt you that won't leave a mark."

Rachel turned to watch the man, blocking the woman's view of her right hand. Keeping her movements slow, Rachel took the tape recorder out of her pocket and let her hand drop to her side. The tape recorder slid from her fingers, slipping underneath the car seat.

Before Smithy could open the door, Rachel opened it herself and stood up. "All right, then. What now?"

The woman got out of the car, a dark silhouette against the light from the gate. "Take her to his office. I'll let him know she's here."

It took an effort of will for Rachel not to look back and check if the woman had noticed her hiding the tape recorder. That slim piece of plastic was the only evidence she had to prove her story—and maybe it was a bargaining chip she could use to save her life.

Michael sat in the basement, listening to the mad scientist rant.

He kept his eyes closed. He was not sure when he had regained consciousness, but he had woken to find himself sitting in a chair, handcuffs linking his wrists to the chair arms and his legs bound, as well.

His fingers probed for the hole of the handcuffs that bound his hands together. Not that he had a paper clip or anything else to use to pick the lock.

It was his fault he'd been captured. He'd gotten careless. He had been standing outside his SUV, on the phone with Dr. Green, playing the part of a government official questioning her ability to practice medicine in the state of Oregon. He told her there'd been some allegations of unethical behavior, complaints from former patients in Salem that were being looked into again. The doctor's voice had gone from calm and controlled to high-pitched outrage in an impressively short span of time.

Then Michael caught a glimpse of a man who looked a lot like the driver of the van, the man who'd tried to kidnap Rachel. He'd left his car and gone to check, but the man had turned around the corner. As Michael came up to the corner, he felt a sharp blow on the head.

He had woken to find himself tied to a chair in one corner of some kind of laboratory. That's how he thought of it, though it didn't look much like his old chemistry lab in high school.

Instead of Bunsen burners and flasks, strange machines flashed and beeped. Unidentifiable fluids bubbled through long glass cylinders and flowed from one tube to another. The only thing he recognized was the emergency shower in the corner, ready to be used in case of a chemical spill.

People in white lab coats were talking in low voices about drug reaction times and absorption levels and a lot of other things way out of Michael's wheelhouse. But he understood enough. He was in trouble.

No one paid any attention to him, so Michael lowered his eyelids to slits. He could only see a small part of what was going on. He took care to breathe slowly and evenly.

What Michael had at first taken for a crowd of people resolved itself into just two figures. A man in a white lab coat stood in the far corner, tapping into a machine. He barely paid attention to the woman next to him. Michael recognized Dr. Green, even if she had shed her white coat and was neatly dressed in a dark pantsuit with sensible low heels. They probably thought him still unconscious.

"...we needed her willing to help us. You were a fool to force her into the van. It made her feel threatened. That's when she started listening to Sullivan."

"When I reported her becoming resistant to the drug, *she* said the woman should be taken care of." Dr. Green sounded defensive.

"Why you couldn't find someone besides that idiot to help us, I don't understand." The man tapped the machine again. "We're almost there. But I can't put the final pieces together without Nora." He turned, and Michael shut his eyes. He had seen enough.

Christopher Vance, the owner of the facility that Nora had worked for. Michael had never liked him, not when Michael came by the lab to pick up Nora for a date and not now. The man was too erratic, a slippery combination of blusteringly arrogant and easily distracted. A rich kid with a lot of toys to play with, who didn't mind if he blew up the toy store so long as it made a nice bang.

"Well," Dr. Green said. "At least I made sure Pete and his friend took that irritating man out of circulation. I called them to pick Nora up. But they found him outside, causing trouble. I figured we couldn't let him hang around asking questions."

"But you lost Nora."

"I told *her* that the girl was missing, and she said she'd take care of it."

Michael had lost the thread of the conversation. He needed time to get his bearings before he could form a plan.

Footsteps crossed the room, stopping just before him. Dr. Vance said petulantly, "Why is he still asleep? What did you give him?"

"I gave him a brief sedative." Cold fingers touched his skin. Michael forced himself not to twitch as Dr. Green checked his pulse. "It should not be keeping him asleep this long."

"Never mind." Dr. Vance made one of his usual abrupt changes of mood. "Let him sleep. We don't need him yet."

Yet.

A whoosh of air came from off to Michael's left as a door opened. Heavier footsteps stomped across the room and Michael heard the voice of the sheriff that Rachel had called Tony. He sounded furious. "What are you doing? You planted that newspaper cutting so I would go along with your plan to have this man arrested by the state police. And now it turns out that not only is he not a criminal but he *is* actually a US marshal? I thought Rachel was confused after the ordeal of her kidnapping, but she was right. And you have actually *abducted* the man? Are you crazy?" Tony's voice rose on the last words. "You have unleashed a whole world of trouble on yourself. All you can do now is let him go and prepare for the consequences."

Dr. Green interjected viciously, "If anything happens to this project, you will be implicated, as well. Don't forget that."

"You wanted to pay me on the side to keep an eye on a sick woman. I didn't have a problem with that. I thought you were trying to help her. I don't know what kind of game you're trying to play here, but I'm not going to go along with anything illegal."

Michael had always considered the Sleepy Cove sheriff merely in the light of an obstacle, and a bit of a fool into the bargain, but there was something admirable about the little man standing up for what he believed in.

The door opened again. High heels tapped across the floor. Then a woman's voice, smooth and unruffled. "We are interested in helping people, as well. This medicine will save thousands of lives, if not millions. And if something happens to interfere with that, it would be…unfortunate. So stay quiet, and let us do our job."

The sheriff demanded, "Was Rachel ever sick in the first place? Or is that just another game that you've been playing?"

Dr. Green said, "We can discuss this in the morning. You are becoming overwrought. You need to calm down. Let me escort you out to your car."

"I'm not going anywhere until I know what is going on here."

The smooth-voiced woman said, "We'll give you a full report tomorrow. Everything will be cleared up by then."

Silence, broken only by the sound of the sheriff breathing heavily. Then, "Fine. You do that. Don't bother seeing me to the door. I can find my own way out."

Michael heard the door open and shut. Then the smooth woman said, "I think you are going to want to see something. I've brought you a present. I know how you like that."

"You're being very mysterious," Dr. Vance

remarked. "Are you trying to arouse my curiosity?"

"Of course. Bring Dr. Green. We may need her."

Their footsteps moved off, and Michael was left alone. He wrestled with the handcuffs. He could stand, after a fashion, with the chair dragging down his balance, and hop a few paces. It was awkward, but he could manage it.

He turned his back and groped at the handle of a drawer. Searched clumsily through the drawers under the counter looking for something, anything, that he could use to pick the lock on the handcuffs. Not even a paper clip. He gritted his teeth and kept looking.

The only positive sign from the conversation he had heard was that they had not spoken of Rachel as if she were injured or worse. She must have escaped the doctor's office, after all. He was fiercely glad. If they injured her, they would pay. He would make sure of it.

The door opened, and Michael froze where he was hunched over the counter. Tony stood in the doorway. He looked furious, his face very red and sweating. He came in and shut the door behind him. Keeping his voice low, he said, "I went down the hall and waited around a corner until I could be sure they weren't coming back. Are you really a marshal?"

Michael lowered the chair to the ground and sat. "Yes," he said cautiously.

"How am I supposed to know if that's actually the case? I couldn't believe it when Doc Green told me. It's gotten to where I don't know what's true anymore and what is a lie."

"Welcome to the club," Michael muttered. Aloud, he said, "If you look in my jacket pocket, you should find my wallet and my ID."

Tony looked through the wallet. "Seems legit."

"It is."

"Huh." Tony stood back and surveyed him. "And what are you doing with Rachel?"

Michael held on to his patience. Tony was his one hope to get out of this alive. "I was trying to keep her safe. I do not know what these people have told you about what they're doing. But I think they mean to harm her. Nora. You call her Rachel. They have messed with her memory. They've given her drugs and brainwashed her into thinking she is someone else."

He saw Tony's eyebrows shoot up toward his hairline and added, "I am not making this up. It's the truth."

Tony handed the wallet back to Michael. "If

I had heard this story last week, I would've said you were crazy. Now, I don't know. They are up to something. And it's not good. When I found out you really were a marshal, I told Doc it had to stop. She said if I turned them in, I'd go to prison, too. She insisted that I drive her here." Tony took out a key and unlocked the handcuffs. "Apparently, she thought once I knew how extensive the setup was, I'd go along with their scheme."

Michael rubbed his wrists. "Sounds like it had the opposite effect." He bent down and unwound the cord that bound his legs.

"I don't know how much help it is to let you loose. There's an electric fence around the perimeter, and there's only one gate. Guards check everyone coming in and going out. I've got a valid pass that will let me through the gates, but I can't get anyone else out."

"I don't want to get out. I want to make them regret they ever let me in the doors. But I need to do something first." Michael searched his pockets. "They took my cell phone. Let me use yours."

"They jam cell phones in here. They're very security conscious. They don't want any industry secrets being stolen. This place is locked up better than Fort Knox."

"Excellent." Michael bared his teeth in a fierce grin. "I can use that."

He took out a card from his wallet and handed it to Tony. "This has the contact information from Detective Wright. He's an investigator with the state police. If you tell him what's going on, he will bring in the police."

"If he believes me," Tony said. "This whole thing sounds unreal even to me, and I know it's the truth."

"Wait. I have a better idea." Michael took back the card and scribbled a phone number on the back. "Call my boss, as well. Tell him I am locked in here, being held hostage. The state police might think this story is some kind of hoax, but Lynch will back you up. He trusts me." He handed the card back. "I'll find a safe place to hide until the police come."

"It's a crazy idea," Tony said. "But I can't think of anything better. Here. You're going to need this." He took his gun out of his holster and handed it to Michael.

"Thanks. They took mine while I was out." Michael looked Tony up and down. "You're going to catch some flak for having helped these criminals in the first place. Can I trust you to call the authorities? It's your duty."

Tony gave a brief bark of a laugh. It held

very little humor. "I guess I can see why you'd feel like you should give me a lecture on my duty. They waved a fat wad of cash in front of me, and I decided to go along. I mean, at first it seemed like they were trying to avoid red tape and excess paperwork, using an experimental drug to help Rachel's issues. I'm a cop. I know that sometimes you have to cut corners to get the job done. But they've gone too far, crossed the line into harming people. It wasn't like that at first. Rachel..." Tony shook his head. "She looked so scared when she first came to town. I honestly thought I was helping her. Never mind that. Now I know better. Whatever I get, I earned. And it doesn't matter, not in the grand scheme of things. Regardless of what happens to me, I'm going to fix this. I reckon I owe it to her." He took the card. "I'll do whatever it takes to get her out of this mess. What about you?"

Michael looked the man straight in the eye. "I love her. I want to marry her."

"Oh." Tony seemed taken aback. "And, er, does she feel the same about you?" He must have seen Michael's expression change, for he said, "Oh, man. That's harsh."

Michael shrugged, faking an indifference he did not feel. Tony added, "But that's not what

I meant. I have to leave soon. If not, they'll start searching the facility to see why I'm still hanging around. If you stay here, will you keep Rachel safe?"

Michael's thoughts shuddered to a complete halt, like a high-speed train performing an emergency braking to avoid running into a landslide. "What do you mean?"

"Rachel," Tony repeated. "She's here in the facility. I just saw them bring her in. I don't think she saw me."

"Change of plan," Michael said grimly.

ELEVEN

The security guard took her to an office. Various awards lined one wall and an enormous desk filled most of the room. He pointed to a chair in front of the desk. "Sit."

Rachel didn't see she had many options. She sat. The man took up a position in front of her. He stared down at her as if looking at a cockroach.

Closing her eyes, Rachel tried to sort out the various impressions. The place smelled familiar. Sharp, chemical, antiseptic scents. She wasn't sure she could describe the precise components but the smells connected instantly with some memory bank in the back of her mind. Not a pleasant memory, judging by the way her pulse raced and her nerves tightened like a bow about to snap.

The door clicked. Rachel opened her eyes to find Dr. Green's sour face peering at her from across the desk. Rachel jumped, pushing back against the chair she found herself in.

"What have you done with my tape recorder, dear?"

"Oh, have you lost it? That might be awkward the next time you have to dictate your notes. Perhaps you put it in the wrong place by mistake. Corrie always keeps putting down her glasses and then I have to hunt all over until I find them."

Dr. Green's sallow cheeks flushed red. "I'm going to find it sooner or later, dear. If you want to stay out of trouble, you'll tell me where it is. Now."

Dr. Green was watching Rachel intently, her dark eyes tracking every small reaction on her face. "How does being back here make you feel?"

Rachel held up her hand. "Please. I have had enough of your stories. And I am not your *dear*. If you're not going to tell me the truth, then don't bother trying to lie." She did not know where she'd found the courage to confront Dr. Green directly. Perhaps it was the shock of hearing the audiotape, or maybe it was the new setting that she found herself in that made her feel like new ground rules could be followed.

"That doesn't sound like the Rachel I knew."
Dr. Green regarded her with satisfaction. "I expect you feel different now, don't you? Things are starting to come back. You are starting to remember things."

Dr. Green was at least partially right. Rachel *was* starting to remember things. But she could still remember being Rachel, her life in Sleepy Cove with people she had thought were her friends.

Maybe…maybe becoming Nora would not destroy her, as she had feared. Michael could be right, regaining Nora's memories could make her complete. She could have had a future with him. It was a pity she'd never get the chance to tell him so.

Now as she looked around the familiar setting, she could remember more and more. That award on the wall, the one with Dr. Vance's name written in a large ornate script. She had been at that award ceremony. He had taken credit for her work, and Michael had urged her to challenge him on it. She had not wanted to cause any strife, with things already so tense in the lab. They had argued about that, she and Michael.

Michael. Where was he in all this mess? Was he even alive? *Please, God.* She had been going to save him, and she could not even save herself. Now that she was back in her familiar surroundings, she realized the danger she was in.

What she wanted most right now was to see Michael again. One chance to say goodbye to him. She was not going to survive this. And she hated that she had left things with him thinking that maybe she did not care. *Oh, Lord, help me to see Michael one more time. Even if only to say goodbye.*

From behind her, she heard a man say triumphantly, "Ha!" Dr. Vance came around the desk, Dr. Green stepping back to get out of his way. He settled into his chair and smiled at Rachel.

He was a beanpole of a man, almost as tall as Michael but much skinnier. His narrow face was pale, and his dark eyebrows angled upward, giving him a satirical look even now, when he was looking so pleased with himself. "You owe me an apology. You thought I couldn't give the drug to a human being for months at a time without causing harm. Well, I showed you. You've taken the drug for months. I had Dr. Green monitor you and take regular blood samples for analysis. And look at you! No ill effects at all."

"She did complain of headaches," Dr. Green put in. "Sometimes nausea. And it did become less effective with repeated use."

Dr. Vance waved his hand. "Every drug has some side effects."

"Maybe if I hadn't had to keep giving her the drug orally. Injections would have been easy enough to do while she was in the hypnotic state."

"The drug doesn't work like that. For best effect, it needs a time-delayed release. Besides intravenous doesn't work as well, remember?"

"Of course, I remember," Dr. Green muttered, sullen. "You saw how long that injection lasted, even when I gave her a hypnosis session with it. Barely an hour later she was arguing with me again about being sent to an asylum. I still say the hypnosis sessions worked best. They had an effect on her even once she built up a tolerance."

"The drug worked for months! She had no idea who she was. She believed whatever story you told her. That's enough to prove that I was right."

"That's all you care about," Dr. Green muttered.

"Of course. What else is there?"

Another woman's voice came from the doorway. The saleswoman from the car. "There is a great deal of money at stake, that's what else. We need to get her to witness that she didn't know who she was, that she had no memory of her past life. She'd make a credible witness. No one would doubt the word of the great Dr. Stewart."

The woman's voice positively dripped with poison and malice. Yet...the voice teased at the edges of Rachel's memory. She had heard it somewhere before, and not at a conference, she was sure of it. She just couldn't pin down where. She wanted to turn to look, but not if that meant turning her back on Dr. Green. If the doctor wanted to try to drug her again, Rachel was going to fight it tooth and nail.

The saleswoman continued, "But if she tells people about the side effects, it will cast doubt on all you've achieved. The investors won't like that."

Dr. Vance frowned. "That's very true." He looked at Rachel. "I don't want you to say anything that would make them doubt this drug's success. You did enough damage in that direction already. You are going to tell everybody that I was right."

"Tell who? What are you talking about?" Rachel's heart was pounding so loud she was surprised Dr. Vance couldn't hear it from a few feet away. They could never let her go public with what she'd experienced. All she had to do was mention being abducted and forcibly drugged and they'd all end up in jail for a long, long time. They wanted her to believe that if she cooperated, they'd let her go. But the truth was, sooner or later, they were going to kill her—perhaps after getting a videotaped endorsement of the drug. Unless Rachel could find a way out of this mess and fast.

Dr. Green said, "And where is my tape recorder? Don't give me that innocent look. I know you took it."

"What are you talking about?" Dr. Vance frowned at her.

"The tape recorder I used in the hypnosis sessions. She must have taken it while I was on the phone with that idiot."

"But if that falls into the wrong hands, it would raise some awkward questions." The man transferred his scowl to Rachel. "What have you done with it?"

Rachel just shook her head.

He patted her down, brusque hands searching quickly and efficiently. "It's not on her. So she must have stowed it in the car. I doubt she would have left it by the side of the road before she was picked up. Go search the car."

Dr. Green opened her mouth as if to protest his peremptory tone, but Dr. Vance snapped out, "Don't argue with me. Go."

After she had shut the door behind her, Vance turned back to Rachel. "We're going to put out a press release announcing the new drug. I have just gotten the investors to trust me enough to the point where I can go public. Even if you hadn't started acting all suspicious, I would've had them bring you in. I've proven that this drug is successful, and it's time to start to profit from all my hard work."

"You weren't the only one working hard," the saleswoman said. She moved around into Rachel's line of sight. Rachel gaped.

It was Corrie, but it was Corrie transformed. She wore a tailored suit and high-heeled pumps. The thick black frame glasses had disappeared, and her frizzy hair was sleeked back into a smooth French twist. She was even wearing bright red lipstick and skillfully blended eye shadow that made her eyes look dark and sultry.

Corrie saw Rachel staring at her. The red lips curved into a slow smile that sent chills down Rachel's spine. "Well? What do you think?" Gone was Corrie's soft speech and hesitant manner. This woman was confident, totally in control of the situation.

Rachel could not think of what to say. "You…uh…you look a little different."

Corrie laughed, lightly, but there was a sharper note that Rachel had not heard before. "You don't think I was going to play that idiotic role forever, do you? I gave up several months of my life to make sure that Dr. Vance's prize employee was safe and out of the way. But that's no longer necessary. You are going to be working for the doctor now. You will do everything he says, exactly as he tells you to. Or things will become very unpleasant, Nora."

Rachel blinked up at her innocently. "Who is Nora?"

Methodically, Michael searched each room along the hallway, though every muscle in his body screamed for him to hurry. Time was limited. He had to get Rachel away from Dr. Vance before the cops came. The last thing he needed was to drive that spoiled brat/genius into doing something reckless that might get Rachel killed.

This whole place was dimly lit, only a few

wall lights down the hallway. The effect made him feel as if he'd stumbled into some kind of horror movie. His footsteps whispered down the tile hallway.

His shadow on the wall shifted, changing shape as he approached the nearest wall lamp, growing smaller as he came close, then lengthening, growing denser until it merged with the darkness. Michael gripped the gun in his hand, ready to use.

The hallway finally ended at a staircase, which Michael climbed carefully, pausing at every step to listen. Another hallway. More empty rooms. One room was locked, and Michael's heart skipped a beat. It was a flimsy door lock, easily broken, but all he found was a tiny closet that held janitorial supplies.

As he came closer to the end of the hallway, he heard voices from behind a doorway outlined in light. The crack of light widened as the door began to swing open. Michael caught the sound of several voices, a confusing jumble of people all speaking at once. He thought he recognized Dr. Green's high-pitched tone raised in protest.

Michael darted back to the janitor's closet, pulling the door shut just in time. Footsteps tapped briskly past the door without pausing, the sound fading as the person moved farther away.

Follow them? Or investigate the office?

He stood a better chance going up against a single person. There was no way to know how many people he would face in that office, but it was more than two, at least. Michael slipped out of the closet and moved swift and silent after the lone person.

He reached the corner and peered cautiously around, just in time to see Dr. Green open a door that led to the parking lot. An overhead light came on automatically as she stepped over the threshold. Michael blinked at the harsh bright light. Dr. Green was still in his line of vision. She'd opened the door of a car and was bending down, totally focused on whatever it was she was doing. Perfect. Michael crept closer to the doorway.

More footsteps. Michael stepped back into the shadows of the hallway as a man said, "Something I can help you with?" He wasn't speaking to Michael. He stood just on the edge of Michael's range of vision. All Michael could see were the tips of his boots and a peaked cap.

Dr. Green straightened. "I'm looking for something that woman might have dropped.

A tape recorder." She measured out the size with her hands. "About this big. I can't find it."

"Allow me," the man said politely. His search was a lot more thorough. After a minute, he fished something out from underneath the seat. "Is this it?"

"Yes!" Dr. Green all but snatched the device from his hand. "I *knew* she had it on her. The lying, conniving—well, anyway, thank you." She turned back to the door, and Michael barely had time to get out of sight behind the door as she swept past.

The security guard did not follow her inside. Presumably, he was making rounds on a regular schedule. Whatever the reason, Michael did not question it. He caught up to Dr. Green in a few swift strides. The woman sensed his presence and started to turn. "Smithy, I don't need your help to—oh!"

Michael covered her mouth with his hand. "Then perhaps you can help me instead." He took the tape recorder from her pocket. It must have something valuable on it, or Rachel would not have tried to hide it. He could only hope it was enough to send this whole crowd away for a long time.

In a few minutes, he left Dr. Green bundled into the janitor's closet, gagged and tied with bandages from a first aid kit. He didn't try to knock her out. All that nonsense on TV about knocking someone on the head to make them lose consciousness briefly and safely had always annoyed him. If that were all it took, there wouldn't be a need for hospitals to use anesthesia. Concussion was brain damage, and it was tricky to gauge the amount you could hit someone without causing permanent harm.

No one could hear Dr. Green's muffled calls unless they came within a few feet of the closet. If the security guard patrolled the grounds on a regular schedule, as he suspected, he had at most an hour or two before someone came down that corridor and heard Dr. Green.

But then his whole life was built on a series of ifs right now, like a deck of cards that could collapse with the least breath of wind. If no one heard Dr. Green. If no one thought to check in the lab and find him missing. If Tony could get someone to listen to him.

Dr. Green hadn't told him much, but he'd learned enough. It warmed his heart to think of Rachel standing up for herself in front of all of them. If Dr. Vance or Corrie tried to hurt Rachel, he'd have to step in. It was risky. If one of them had a gun, as well, Rachel could get hurt. No. It was safer to wait. He had to play for time until Tony brought help.

He moved softly down to the outline of light from all the way at the end of the hall. The office where Rachel was being kept. It crossed his mind that perhaps he should be going the other direction. If he made his way to the front of the compound, flagged down a police officer, he could provide enough probable cause for them to raid the place. End the standoff before Dr. Vance had the opportunity to lawyer up.

But no. He had to make Rachel his top priority. They could kill her before the cops ever got in the door. No way to predict which way a mad scientist in a tight corner would jump.

TWELVE

"I don't know why you're calling me Nora. My name is Rachel Garrett. I think you must have me confused with someone else."

Rachel might be backed into a corner, with few weapons at her disposal, but she had this one. And even trapped as she was, kidnapped and held against her will, she had to admit that watching their reaction was extremely satisfying.

"She is lying," Corrie snapped. Anger flushed her pale cheeks to bright red. The scarlet color clashed with the crimson lipstick. "Don't believe her. It's all an act. She's recovered her old memories, I'm sure of it. The drug has been wearing off for weeks now."

Rachel let a quaver of fear into her voice as she said, "Corrie, what are you talking about? Why aren't you back at the café? What am I doing here?"

"The café has been closed, permanently. And I've had enough games. Do you think I enjoyed being stuck in that hick town baby-sitting you? I'm not going to waste more time watching you trying to play me."

Dr. Vance smirked. "But, Corrie, you were so good at acting the part of a flaky old maid."

Corrie gave him a dirty look. She transferred that look to Rachel. "Well? Do you remember who I am?"

"She might not remember you in any case," Dr. Vance said. "You were only here a month or so before she was taken away. Nora probably never had any reason to meet my assistant. She spent most of her time in the lab."

"Oh, we met." Corrie's lips thinned into a smile with little humor. "The great Dr. Stewart didn't appreciate my way of dealing with one of her lab workers. Seemed to think I was too harsh. We had…words. She'll remember that. Don't you, Doctor?"

The incident sounded vaguely familiar, though Rachel could not recall any details. She was careful not to let any recognition show on her face. "Of course, I remember you, Corrie. I work for you."

"Yes." Corrie smirked. "I did enjoy being the one to give *you* orders. The great high-

and-mighty scientist sweeping the floor every night. Used to drop a pie on the floor sometimes just for the satisfaction of watching you kneel down at my feet to clean up the mess."

Dr. Vance broke in, clearly impatient with this gloating. "I assigned Corrie to watch over you when you were stuck in that town. Had to change her appearance, of course. Didn't want to risk sparking a memory. The glasses were my idea."

"They never fit right," Corrie muttered. "Kept falling down my nose."

Dr. Vance ignored this. "You were so insistent, so convinced that the side effects hadn't been investigated thoroughly enough. I knew you were going to cause trouble with the FDA if I didn't stop you. I can't wait until you get your memory back fully so you remember those arguments. I want to hear you tell me that I was right."

The doctor rocked forward on his toes, jubilant. He was like a little boy who'd just pulled off a successful prank. "What better way to prove that the drug was safe than to use it on the one person who needed convincing? And it did work. I was right." He waved a hand. "Granted, it was a bit tricky to set things up, finding a doctor willing to monitor your progress and getting you the right paperwork to pass in society. But once that was done, the rest just fell into place. No one questioned a thing. The only snag in the whole setup was we had to make sure someone was on hand to check that you took your pills every day without fail."

"And whenever you missed taking them for a day or two, you went back to talking like a science nerd," Corrie interjected. "Do you have any idea how annoying that was to listen to?"

"I'm sorry, Corrie, but I don't have the faintest idea what you are talking about."

Corrie almost snarled with frustration. She leaned forward, putting her hands on the chair arms. With her face inches from Rachel, she said, "I'm getting tired of these games. Even if you're not faking this little-miss-innocent act, and even if you don't believe in this wonder drug—and how very rich it is going to make us—maybe there's another way to convince you." Her red lips curved in an evil smile. "We've got your precious boyfriend locked up here. If you want to keep him alive and well, then you'll do exactly as we say."

Dr. Vance led Rachel down a flight of stairs and down another endless hallway before he pushed open a door and ushered her into a much larger room. Rachel looked around.

White walls, steel tables and a sense of familiar dread. The lab. An overwhelming wave of despair washed over her. Yes. This was where it had all begun to go wrong.

"Where is he?" Corrie looked around and cursed. "It might have been that fool of a sheriff. I knew you shouldn't have trusted him."

Wild hope leaped inside Rachel's chest, like a bird set free. Could Michael have escaped? With Tony? The thought warmed her even in this dark situation. At least one friend from Sleepy Cove had actually been one of the good guys, after all.

"It doesn't matter. We have Nora. She's the key to this whole situation." Dr. Vance spoke breezily, but Rachel knew him well enough to see the worry that lay beneath the bravado. He shoved Rachel into a chair. She did not resist. Perhaps she could defuse the situation before he did something reckless. She sat still and folded her hands, waiting for the right moment.

The landline in the corner buzzed. Frowning, Corrie answered it. "Yes?"

A brief murmur on the other end of the line. Rachel could not distinguish the words, but the urgency was unmistakable. When Corrie came back, the frown was more pronounced. She stopped in front of Rachel, a hand on her hip, fashionable shoe rotated out in fifth position like a model. "The police are at the gate," she announced. "Apparently, someone told them that we were holding people incommunicado."

Dr. Vance swung around to stare at Rachel. She spread her hands out, innocent. "I didn't call them. Dr. Green took my phone away, remember? Said it was the cause of too much stress."

It must have been Tony who called the police. Not that his interference was likely to help her present situation.

Dr. Vance waved at Corrie. "Go hold them off. Play for time until I can convince Nora. It won't take very long."

Corrie said sourly, "You sound very sure of yourself."

"I am. You see, I have one more card to play in this little game."

Corrie went.

Rachel said quietly, "What are you planning to do?"

"It's simple enough," Dr. Vance said. "Another injection of the drug to wipe out your short-term memories. A quick hypnosis session on who you are and why you're here. Make it convincing enough, and the police will think you came here of your own accord and there's nothing wrong." He took out a vial from the small refrigerator in the back of the lab. "This dosage is stronger than the previous version. It should last long enough."

"No," Rachel said. "Please." She had reached the end of the line, it seemed. No amount of acting was going to get her out of this situation.

Dr. Vance looked at her, no emotion at all on his hard face. For a moment, Rachel dared to hope. He was merciless when someone got between him and his goal, but he did need her alive and with her memory intact. Perhaps...

Dr. Vance took a step forward. "Stay still," he ordered.

Rachel took another step back. "You have no idea how much it hurts to lose everything you know. To have everyone you think you can trust turn out to be lying to you."

"You'll feel much better in a few minutes." Dr. Vance smiled at her, a mirthless smile like a skeleton grinning. "I promise."

Michael cracked the door open. The office was brightly lit. It was also completely deserted. Rachel was gone. He turned around in the hallway. At the far end, he could see the lighted outline of another room. Cautiously, he made his way down the hall and pressed his ear against the door, straining to hear.

A faint movement of air behind him was his only warning. He spun around and saw the woman raising a gun in his direction. Before she could react, he grabbed her wrist, forcing her arm up and twisting her wrist so that she was forced to release the gun. He grabbed it and backed up, keeping the weapon pointed at her.

The woman he'd known as Corrie rubbed her wrist, looking at him sourly. "Very clever, Mr. US Marshal. Now what?"

"Now we go talk to Vance. See how valuable you are to him."

Corrie snorted. "You think you can walk in there with a gun to my head and order Vance to let Nora go? He'll never do it. I know him. He'll never admit that he can't have whatever he wants, and what he wants is for Nora to help prove that he's still the child prodigy everyone predicted would get a Nobel Prize before he was thirty. He's too old for that now, but he still can't give up on the idea of being recognized as a genius. He's wanted that all his life. It's all he wants. If you ask him to give up on that dream, he'll kill Nora."

Unfortunately, that sounded like an accurate assessment of Vance's personality, from what he recalled. "But if he shoots her, it's all over. He loses. There's no way he'd achieve his dream of being a success then."

"No," Corrie said. Her eyes were steady on Michael's face, reading every nuance of expression. "Not exactly. He wouldn't be known for his scientific discoveries, but he'd still be notorious. A man like that wants attention, no matter the cost. But Nora would still be dead. And you'd have to go on living, knowing you could have stopped him."

Oh, she was good. This woman was the sort who could sell sand at the beach. He couldn't fault her logic, dearly as he wanted to. He tried to rally. "Then I'll take you with me to talk to the cops. We'll let them in, and *they* can explain matters to Vance."

"And he'll shoot Nora before they can break down the lab door." Corrie remained calm. "You can't beat him by force. He holds all the cards."

"I'm not going to let him kill Nora."

"There's only one thing you can do to save her," Corrie said. "Your life for hers. Do you love her enough for that?"

When Michael walked into the lab, Rachel was backed up against the counter. She caught sight of Michael and for a moment her face lit up with relief. Then she saw the woman behind him, and she froze. It was worse than anything, to know he'd failed her. "Hi, honey. Sorry I missed you back in Sleepy Cove."

The woman waved him into a chair. He sat, keeping his gaze fixed on Rachel.

"Corrie, what are you doing here?" Vance kept his arm on Rachel. "Why aren't you talking to the police? Did you get rid of them already?"

"They won't talk to me. I'm not important enough. They have to talk to the boss. And they're getting pretty tired of waiting. You'd better go out there and settle things down. I'll keep an eye on them."

"I was going to drug Nora into telling them everything was fine."

"There's no need to drug her." Corrie prodded Michael with the gun. "The fool is so infatuated with this man that she'll do anything to save him. Won't you, dear?"

"If you shoot him, I'll never work for you," Rachel said passionately. "I don't care what you threaten me with. No amount of hypnosis can convince a person to do something against their will."

"That's true," Dr. Vance allowed. "I couldn't

have had Green hypnotize you into becoming a serial killer or something like that. But I can convince you to do what you have to do to save this man's life."

It troubled Michael that Dr. Vance was talking openly about Michael's fate in front of him. That could only mean that he was planning to kill him—eventually.

"This isn't a good time for you to be noble and self-sacrificing," he said under his breath.

"It's an even worse time for you to die, trust me," Rachel said quietly. "I won't let them hurt you."

"That's very touching," Dr. Vance said impatiently. "But stop stalling. Are you going to cooperate?"

"There's no time for this," Corrie broke in. "You go talk to the police. Stall them for a few minutes. I'll get Nora to do what I say. She's used to it, after these past months."

Dr. Vance held up his hand. "One moment. Nora, you're right. I won't kill him. But I don't have to." He picked up the needle. "I can still take him away from you."

The needle was inches away from Michael's arm. Michael stared at the bright metal point, gleaming in the overhead light. It was like looking over the edge of a cliff into oblivion.

Rachel said shakily, "No. You can't do that to him."

Dr. Vance smiled. "Actually, I can. Is it so wrong to give him a life where he can be happy? I'm not a cruel man. I'll find some nice woman and convince him that he's in love with her, and they can live happily-ever-after. That would make you feel better, I imagine. To know that he's got a nice life with a wife and family and everything a man needs to make his life pleasant? I know a lot of men who'd be banging the door down, trying to get a life like that, and I can arrange it for him right now. I'll do it, Nora. Say the word, and he can live happily-ever-after. Or at least he can have a good life for a few years, until his body builds up a tolerance to the drug."

"And you'd be content to just subsidize his existence somewhere? For months and years? I don't believe you."

"I don't know if I'd need to kill him even then. By that time, he'd be so used to playing the role of a happily married man he probably wouldn't want to stop. I mean, leave a woman who loves him? And all the little kiddies? No, I think he'd be more likely to stay where he was and make the best of it."

Rachel shut her eyes. A tear slid down her

cheek, followed by another. Her voice shaking, she said, "I can't let you kill him."

Dr. Vance nodded, satisfied. He handed the needle to Corrie. "Here. I'll stall the police long enough for Nora to pull herself together and wash her face. In five minutes, I want to see her at the gate smiling and happy." He left.

Corrie reached into a cabinet and took out a couple of padded restraints. "Tie him to the chair. These restraints are padded. It won't hurt."

Still crying, Rachel knelt down to bind Michael's arms to the chair. "I'm so sorry," she whispered. "I'm sorry I didn't trust you enough to take me right out of town the first time we talked. If I'd listened to you then, we wouldn't be here now. But I was too afraid to hear you."

"Don't do it, Rachel." Michael's voice was steady. She opened her eyes to find his eyes on her, as if she were the only person in the room, in the world. "Listen to me. This is my choice. I'd rather die as the man I am than live a false life that someone else chose for me."

"I can't just let you die," Rachel said despairingly.

But Michael shook his head. "Either way, I'm going to die. I get it now, what you were talking about earlier. When you said you'd rather die as the Rachel you knew than change into someone else."

Corrie relaxed as Rachel finished binding Michael. "Stand away from him. I'm not bluffing," Corrie said. "I'll kill him if you say no."

Rachel backed away, and Corrie relaxed. "That's better." She slipped the gun into her jacket pocket and picked up the vial. Michael watched as the needle filled with the clear liquid. It looked so harmless, but he knew he was looking into oblivion.

Corrie looked up. "Why are you standing there? Do you want to watch me inject him?"

Rachel shook her head helplessly. "If you drug him, he'll forget ever knowing me. At least give me a moment to say goodbye."

"There's no time to argue now," Corrie said briskly. "If you stall, the police will get a search warrant and find Michael. But they'll find a man who doesn't know his own name. How much faith can they put in the testimony of a man who's having memory issues? A woman who ran away and lived under an alias for months? There's no proof that you didn't leave voluntarily. It's your word against mine."

Rachel hesitated, looking at Michael. His heart leaped. That wasn't the look of a woman who didn't want anything to do with him. That was the look of a woman who loved him.

Was he fooling himself? Maybe, but if that was going to be his last memory of Rachel, he'd take it.

Then her gaze moved past him, and her lips parted as if struck by a thought. "Corrie, do you know the penalty for assaulting a US marshal?" Rachel's eyes flicked to Michael and then back to the corner of the room.

Almost imperceptibly, hoping he was reading her correctly, Michael nodded.

Corrie started to say, "What are you talk—"

Before she could finish the question, Michael was on his feet. Still bound to the chair, he thrust his shoulder against Corrie's arm. The needle went flying. Corrie grabbed for the gun, but Rachel was already pushing her into the corner, beneath the emergency shower. Rachel jerked at the handle and several gallons of water rushed out, drenching Corrie, straight in the face with tremendous force, blinding her. She dropped the gun and cried out in pain.

Michael waited in agonized impatience while Rachel retrieved the gun from the floor and bent to untie him, while in the corner Corrie covered her eyes with her hands, moaning in pain and shock.

Finally. Michael was freed from that insufferable chair. It was a glorious feeling. After those last few minutes, looking over the cliff, he felt back in control of his life.

Gently, he drew Rachel toward him and wrapped his arms around her until she stopped shaking. Then he dropped a light kiss on her forehead. "Thank you for rescuing me."

"We rescued each other." Rachel still sounded shaky, but a healthy color had returned to her cheeks. She stepped back, and he missed her warmth, but she made up for it by giving him a broad smile. "You're safe. *We* are safe. Everything is going to be all right now."

He touched her cheek. "Come on. Let's tie up your friend and go have a word with the police."

THIRTEEN

It was over. The police had come—steely-eyed men who took reports and photographed the laboratory and took away evidence. They had led Dr. Vance off, still volubly protesting how they didn't understand the importance of his great discovery. A sour Dr. Green followed afterward and Corrie, still rubbing her reddened eyes.

For the second night in a row, Michael was kept busy answering questions for hours. He gave a report to the state police, to his boss and even to Parker, who showed up, tired but grinning, as dawn began to spread daylight over the eastern hills.

At some point in all this, Rachel disappeared. "She's fine," Parker assured Michael, as they sat in Vance's office with Lynch. "Lynch called me in to talk with her. I wanted her to go to the hospital to be checked out.

She's not that fond of doctors, and I can't blame her, but we need to make sure no side effects lingered from all the drugs she'd been given."

"Makes sense. Where is she? Which hospital?"

"Eugene General. I'm going there now to check on her."

"You can give me a ride." Michael started to get to his feet.

"Hold on there." Michael's boss waved him back into his chair. Lynch was a big bear of a man, with grizzled hair going gray and a deep voice that commanded obedience. His gruff manner hid a kind demeanor, but his orderly nature balked at the chaotic mess Michael had dropped in his lap. "You're not going anywhere. There's still a lot more we need to sort out here. We found Nora's purse and personal effects still in her office down the hall." Lynch shoved a box over the desk toward Michael. "Including her engagement ring."

Michael took the box. "I suppose they were trying to maintain the illusion that she took a leave of absence to sell her participation in this scheme."

"Probably. Vance is claiming that she willingly agreed to take the drug and develop amnesia, you know."

Michael scoffed, "No one would do that."

Parker said, "I don't know if I'd say that. Some people would quite like to have a clean break from their past, a fresh start in life."

"Maybe, but I don't think Sullivan's girlfriend is one of them," Lynch said.

"If she *is* my girlfriend. That's one of the things I need to sort out. The last time I spoke to her before I got captured by those thugs... she wasn't very happy with me."

"I still want to get all this clear," Lynch grumbled. "It's hard to believe it could be that easy to change someone's own sense of identity."

"I don't think you need to worry about a crime wave of, um, identity theft of this sort," Parker said. "Without steady access to this new drug, they could never have robbed Nora of her memory at the start. And while the drugs and hypnosis strategy worked early on, things started to fall apart soon enough. They made enough mistakes that her subconscious started to question what was going on. Then when she started to feel uneasy, each oddity only reinforced the sense that something was wrong."

Michael clenched his fist. "So that's why Dr. Green kept increasing the frequency of the hypnosis sessions."

"In time, she would have been able to fight off the illusions they'd spun on her own without any help," Parker concluded.

"And no one in that town she was living in ever figured out that something was wrong?" Lynch sounded incredulous.

Parker shrugged. "People see what they expect to see. And Rachel acting afraid made it all the more credible that she was suffering from nervous anxiety. As indeed she was—but not from organic causes. I hope they put this crowd away for a very long time."

"All except Tony," Michael said. "He actually did figure out that something was wrong. Took him a long time to do it, but still. If it hadn't been for Tony getting the word out, I don't think Rachel or I would have made it out of that lab. I'll testify on his behalf if he needs me."

Lynch shifted in his chair. "I don't think you need to worry about that sheriff. He's going to stay here in Eugene tonight—looks like he's got a lot of explaining to do. But I doubt they'll find anything to charge him with."

Michael said, "Maybe if he's going back to Sleepy Cove in the morning, he can give me a ride out there. I still haven't found out what that Dr. Green did with my car."

His boss grumbled, "I suppose this means you're going to take another week off to straighten things out."

Michael shook his head. "I'm not going to get you into trouble. I'll resign, if that's what you need. I'm grateful for your help convincing the state police that we were in physical danger. You saved my life, and Rachel's, with your intervention."

"You've saved mine before," Lynch said. He looked at Michael for a long moment. Michael was not sure what Lynch could read on his face, but his boss's grim expression softened slightly. "Unfortunately, in my absence, Josh seems to have piled stacks of papers all over my desk. I'm not sure I can find the paperwork that I need to fill out to let you go. Might take me a week or two to locate it under all that mess." His boss took the engagement ring out of Nora's box of belongings and tossed it to him. "And take that ring with you. See if you can return it to its owner. I don't want to leave something like that around in evidence."

Michael caught the ring. "Thanks."

"Just don't think about leaving to talk to her yet," Lynch warned. "There's still a lot more to sort out here. You can sort things out with Nora later."

"Rachel," Michael corrected.

"I'll make sure she's all right," Parker said. "As a friend, not a psychiatrist. I don't know if she's ready to have any psychiatric treatment. If I were in her shoes, it would be a long time before I could allow myself to trust a doctor again. But I want her to know that I'm available to listen, if she needs me."

Michael felt some of the tension ease out of him. "I think she needs to hear that."

Maybe that was what Rachel needed from him, as well. Friendship. It was a far cry from what he wanted, but if that was what she needed, he'd agree to it.

It was late in the day before Michael got a ride to the hospital. He took the time to stop off at his apartment in Eugene to shower and change into clean clothes. He even shaved. This time, she should see him looking his best.

Try as he might, Michael couldn't suppress a twinge of anxiety. What if she still felt the way she had back in Sleepy Cove, when she'd told him they didn't have a future?

The ring was in his pocket now. Michael fingered it nervously. Strange, to pin all his hopes on a thin sliver of metal.

He didn't want to rush her, but when the

time was right, he was going to ask Rachel to marry him. Again. If she rejected him this time, he'd know it wasn't just the dark cloud of fear and doubt that caused her to push him away. This time, it would be final. When he got to the hospital, he went down the hallway toward Rachel's room slowly, delaying the inevitable for a moment.

But the hospital room was empty. A passing nurse told him. "The patient checked out. She went home."

"Oh." He didn't know why he had expected her to tamely wait there until he came to pick her up. "All right, I'll head by her apartment. It's not that far."

The nurse raised her eyebrows. "Sounded like a bit of a drive to me. She said something about going somewhere on the coast, some small town."

Michael had no recollection of making his way out of the hospital, not until he was on the street again. The sun was setting behind the Coast Range hills. The light hit him right in the eyes, blinding him.

He felt blinded in more ways than one. He had been positive that Rachel was ready to move on, to leave Sleepy Cove and accept her old life again. He'd thought she had broken free of her limitations, everything that was holding her back.

Everything that was keeping them apart.

Evidently, he'd been mistaken.

When he got home, he called Parker. Maybe Rachel had said something to him.

"Oh, going back to Sleepy Cove was my idea," Parker said.

"Seriously?" Michael wanted to brain the man. "What were you thinking? She was trapped there for months."

"That's the point," Parker said soberly. "She has so many dark memories of that place. I wanted her to see it from a perspective that wasn't colored by fear. That way, she won't have to deal with nightmares. She needs to face her past and put it into perspective."

But Michael couldn't help wondering, would he be relegated to the past along with all her other nightmares? He needed to see her once more, in the open air and the daylight world, to find out where he stood with Rachel once and for all. He only prayed he wasn't too late.

Gently, Rachel laid the old family Bible into her suitcase on top of the meager collection of clothes and trinkets that were all she owned in Sleepy Cove. Her fingers caressed the Bible's

smooth, worn cover. There was no way to discover whose it had been originally, no name
on the flyleaf, apart from the dedication, and
no way to find out where Corrie had gotten
it. But Rachel decided that wasn't what was
important. Even if it wasn't really a gift from
her family, it still felt right to have it. This
Bible had been part of someone's family once.
Maybe it could be part of a family again. Hers.
If Michael—she closed the suitcase as though
she could shut that train of thought off before
it got started again.

Michael. He was the problem.

She had not heard from him, hadn't seen
him. When she had tried to phone him this
morning, to see if she could arrange a time and
place to meet, his phone had either been turned
off or was outside of calling range.

For a man who had spent so much time
stalking her, he was annoyingly absent when
she most wanted to talk to him. Some things
she couldn't express properly over the phone.
She had to find a way to meet with him face-
to-face.

It troubled her that she could not contact
him. Had she lost her opportunity?

Looking back, she probably should have
spoken with him that night in the lab. But at

the time, he had been surrounded by police and various officials. A serious discussion about where their relationship stood would have felt rushed and awkward. After all the trauma, they needed a chance to step back and regroup.

She had managed to get a chance to talk to Dr. Parker. At first, Rachel hadn't recognized the tall, thin man with the untidy salt-and-pepper hair, just one more stranger in the crowd of law enforcement that had swarmed through the lab. But once he spoke, she recognized his warm, smooth voice instantly. It felt like meeting an old friend again, though she had never met him before.

Dr. Parker looked around the lab. "So, do you remember this place? Your work here?"

Rachel hesitated. "It's coming back but it's strange. I can't quite describe it. I can remember the time I spent here, though it still feels like something that happened to someone else. Like a transparent layer over existing memories. Yet I also remember all the months I spent thinking I was merely Rachel Garrett. I remember my time in Sleepy Cove, but I also remember working in the lab."

She looked down at the floor, feeling shy. "I remember Michael." Then hurriedly, she went on, "But I thought I was going to forget everything about my time in Sleepy Cove. That was what had happened to those other people who suffered from this kind of amnesia."

Thankfully, Parker did not ask her what she remembered about Michael. Rachel knew she shouldn't have blurted that out. It was too soon. The rush of old memories was too new. She needed time to process everything. At the moment, she needed more than anything to catch her balance, feel as if the ground under her feet had become steady again.

Parker said, "I don't think it's surprising that your case is different from the documented cases of dissociative amnesia. When people develop this type of amnesia organically, it seems to come from a need to escape an intolerable situation. You weren't like that. Since the drug only mimicked the symptoms without the underlying cause, it makes sense it wouldn't behave exactly the same."

"I hope some good can come out of this. Dr. Vance was right about how this drug could help people who need to deal with trauma. So long as it's used with their consent and understanding." Wrath filled her. "And no one gets any false memories planted of people who never existed."

It still rankled, the false story of growing

up on an isolated farm, of having lived all the joys and sorrows of a childhood that had never existed. She still remembered the day her father had taken her out to the river and she had caught her very first trout. The memory was so real she could almost taste it.

Perhaps in time the strength of these false memories would fade. It helped that she could also now remember her real parents, with their dearly loved faces. Her childhood back east, her job in Oregon. Meeting Michael.

Two lives, lived in parallel. She told Parker, "I'm still divided into two people, but now I know what's been going on. I think it will all work out in the long run."

"So you're going to stay on, keep the facility going?"

"I'm not sure about that," Rachel said. "This place was run with the money Dr. Vance got from investors. They might not want me to work on it."

"They'd be fools if they didn't," Dr. Parker said. "From the sound of it, you were the only person aside from Vance who understood every aspect of this drug."

"Even if they don't want me to keep working here, I want to stay in Eugene, anyway."

"Ah. That would put you into frequent contact with Michael. So…are you comfortable with that?"

"No," Rachel said honestly. "Comfortable is not the right word." Her emotions still all tumbled about inside her, raw and intense. And above all, private. She didn't want to discuss her feelings with anyone but Michael himself.

When Rachel drove out to Sleepy Cove, she had parked her rental car just past the city limits. That was deliberate. She needed to prove to herself that she could walk out of town in broad daylight, when she wasn't fueled by desperation and terror. The nightmare was over, and she was back in the sane and sunlit world.

As Rachel walked down Main Street for the final time from her apartment, she took a last look around.

Nothing had changed. Sleepy Cove was still an innocent, quaint little town. It no longer held any sinister shadows. In the bright sunshine and with the shroud of fear no longer tinting her vision, the pretty Victorian facades still looked like a postcard come to life, and the tourists still wandered from shop to shop, eager for novelty T-shirts and saltwater taffy.

Only she had changed. Rachel no longer felt that she had to settle for being frightened all the time. She had been tried in a crucible of fear and come out stronger in her faith.

The Blue Whale Café still had the old closed sign hanging in the window, but through the glass Rachel could see there was a pleasant hive of activity going on inside.

A hand touched her elbow, a light, tentative touch. Miss Trant stood there, her wrinkled face anxious. "It's good to see you again, Rachel. You're looking well. Not so jumpy anymore, eh?"

"No." Rachel smiled at Miss Trant reassuringly. "I'm feeling much better."

"I'm so glad." The older lady's face relaxed a bit, though she did not look entirely at ease. "That nice man at the bakery told me that the woman who runs the saltwater taffy shop told him that Tony told *her* that something was wrong with Dr. Green's treatment. I was very sorry to hear that."

Rachel followed the tortuous line of communication perfectly. Typical Sleepy Cove. "I've stopped taking the medication she was giving me. It turned out it wasn't as helpful as she thought it would be."

"I went by her cottage the other day to see if she wanted to contribute to the local charity drive, but her place was all boarded up, with a for-lease sign on it. Is it true she's closed up shop and isn't going to be doing business here any longer?"

"Dr. Green is not going to be practicing medicine anywhere, not ever. She's lost her license."

Miss Trant shook her head, puzzled. "It's all very confusing. I know you always had trusted her. And certainly, she *seemed* like a nice person. But so many other odd things were happening that I started to wonder if there wasn't something wrong there, after all. I'm only sorry you had to suffer, dear. I always thought doctors wanted to help people. I don't know why people have to do such wicked things."

"Most doctors do try." The older lady looked so woebegone, Rachel patted her shoulder reassuringly. "Dr. Green was a rare exception."

"Oh, I forgot, Tony said you were some kind of doctor yourself. Is that right? It sounded very confusing, the whole story."

"It was confusing, at least at the time. But I think everything is going to be all right now." Rachel nodded toward the window that now had the words *Blue Whale Café* stenciled across the glass. Inside, contractors hammered on the final pieces of the refurbished counter or stood on ladders painting the walls a light cornflower blue. "I see you've started the renovation work already."

"Oh, yes," Miss Trant said more brightly. "I don't know why I didn't think of it sooner. I'm getting bored with the whole idea of retirement, and Mrs. Benson thought it really would be nice if there was a place people could gather to chat and catch up on their lives, especially if it stayed open all afternoon." She smiled at Rachel, awkwardly. "I only wish the renovations were a little further along, so I could ask you in for a cup of coffee. Still, if you have time, perhaps you could come by for tea at my cottage?"

"I have had enough tea to last me a lifetime." Corrie drugging her tea was another memory Rachel was going to have to work hard to get over. She was not fully healed, not yet. But she was getting better.

Mrs. Gibbs came bustling up, her hands filled with rolls of wallpaper samples. "Helena, dear, are you sure you wanted the painters to use that color on the walls? I thought we'd agreed on a nice floral wallpaper in pink and cream."

Mrs. Benson followed her, clutching a chartreuse fabric swatch. "*We* never agreed on anything of the sort, *dear*. I hardly think that two months working as a secretary for an interior designer gives you any particular insight into how to run *our* café."

Mrs. Gibbs made a little humph sound. "Well, working in a library doesn't make you an expert, either."

"Librarians are experts on everything," Mrs. Benson said dryly.

Mrs. Gibbs opened her mouth to retort, then with visible restraint, she turned toward Rachel instead. "Rachel, dear. How lovely to see you back."

Mrs. Benson blinked. "Oh, Rachel! I hardly recognized you for a moment. You seem changed somehow." She frowned. "I'm not sure why. You're still wearing the same clothes, but…there's something different about the way you carry yourself. I can't put my finger on it. But in any case, I'm glad to see you back." A look of determination crossed her face. "Tell me, what do *you* think about the color of the walls?"

Rachel hurriedly disclaimed any opinion of the decorations. On impulse, she gave a quick hug to Mrs. Benson and even a hug to Mrs. Gibbs, who looked surprised but pleased. Then she continued down the street.

Of all the things that Corrie and the others

had done, maybe the worst was to make her believe that the world was a dark place with no one in it that she could trust. It was good to know that she had friends here. With Corrie and Dr. Green gone, no one in Sleepy Cove was her enemy any longer. If she ever came back to this little town, she would find people here still ready to greet her. The thought warmed her, despite the cold wind that blew off the ocean.

She no longer felt the urge to stay here in Sleepy Cove. That compulsion seemed to have been burnt out by the terror of the past few days. But she wanted to leave no room for the sort of doubt that used to plague her when she woke up in the small hours of the morning. Rachel needed to be sure. This last walk was a final check for any lingering anxiety.

As she passed the police station, Tony came out. "I was hoping to catch you before you left." Though the day was not warm, Tony was red-faced and perspiring. He shifted from one foot to another, looking down. He mumbled, "I'm sorry."

"It's all right, Tony." Rachel meant it. "I have to admit, I found it all a bit too much at the time, but I knew you were only trying to help me."

"It's good of you to forgive me," Tony said.

"I'm not so sure I'll find it easy to forgive myself. The whole setup wasn't right. They told me you had become ill and needed help. I should have known better."

"Corrie and Dr. Green were masters at manipulating people to get what they wanted. All the townspeople took them at face value, and they took full advantage of that."

"You can stay." Tony blurted the words out, all in a rush. Then he turned even redder. Gruffly, he said, "You know that, right? I'm sure the ladies would give you a job at the café again. It's a nice town, honestly. I think you could be happy here."

"I'd love to come back and visit, but honestly…my place is somewhere else."

"That's what I thought," Tony said resignedly. "But if you ever change your mind, we'll be here."

Rachel gave him a peck on the cheek. "You're a good man, Tony."

He brushed that aside, but Rachel thought he looked pleased. "You'll be getting that man mad at me."

Rachel's smile faded. "I don't know about that. I still need to talk to him. He was so busy with talking to his boss and the state police that I didn't get a chance before Dr. Parker whisked me off to the hospital for a physical."

Tony shook his head. "He'll wait for you, however long it takes. I misjudged him at first. Spent too much time listening to Corrie's lies. Apparently, she has confessed to phoning in the anonymous tip about Sullivan. After you told her an old friend had rescued you from those men in the van, she asked Vance about any male friends you had. That's how she learned about you being so close to Sullivan and him being a marshal. I guess you'd told people in your lab about Sullivan being involved in the breakup of that isolationist group, so Vance must have told Corrie. She probably figured that the state police would question him long enough for her to get you drugged and kidnapped before he got back."

"She almost got him killed." That was another thing Rachel was going to find hard to forgive. She had come so close to losing Michael forever.

"She almost got both of you killed," Tony said soberly. "Can I give you a ride to your car?"

"No, honestly, I don't want that. It's not that far, and I really need to walk out there by myself."

"Well, okay. I'm sorry to see you leave." He

ducked his head. "And I am sorry for any harm I caused. I honestly thought I was helping you."

"I know." Rachel gave him a quick hug, as well.

Tony patted her shoulder awkwardly. "I guess this is goodbye, then. You take care."

"I will," Rachel promised. "And don't mind me. I don't mind walking by myself."

Tony said, "I don't think you'll be on your own for long." He did not explain his comment, merely stepped back and gave her a nod before turning back to the police station.

It wasn't until Rachel reached the city limits that she understood what Tony had been talking about. Michael was there, leaning against her rental car, his arms folded and his expression inscrutable.

Rachel walked past the city-limits sign without a moment's hesitation. Her heart was beating fast. Not with fear this time. With hope.

She could not just run to Michael and throw her arms around him, dearly as she wanted to. There were things she needed to know first. Such as whether he could accept her as she was, a mixture of her past and present. Only she wasn't sure how to start.

"I had a hunch you'd come out here." Michael tilted his head, indicating her rental car.

"I got a lift out to Sleepy Cove from Tony. Still haven't found out what Dr. Green did with my car after I left it in the alley outside her cottage."

"That's why you came out here? To get your car back?" Rachel squashed down a feeling of disappointment.

"That was the excuse I told myself." Michael straightened up and looked at her directly. "But the truth is, I don't care if I find my car or not. I came because I wanted to see you, talk to you."

"I was hoping to talk with you, as well." Rachel groped for the right words.

Why was it so hard to say what she was really feeling? She wanted to spend her life with Michael. But only if he wanted her, the whole person, not just the woman she had been before. The stay in Sleepy Cove had changed her, for good and ill. It would take time to rebuild her life in Eugene—not as it had been before, but as a mixture of the person she had been and the person she was now.

Michael held himself as stiffly as if facing a firing squad. "So what's the plan now? Where will you go? What will you do?"

"Well…someone told me once to keep my friends close and my enemies closer."

Quietly, he said, "And which am I?"

She took a step forward. Somehow, it was easy now, to reach out and lay her hand on his chest. "Hello, friend," she said softly. "I couldn't say that to you before. I had to come back here, get a sense of closure. I can remember my life as Nora, and I've accepted it, but I can also remember the time I spent living as Rachel. They weren't all bad memories, you know. I had friends here, just as I have in Eugene."

He did not move. "I want to be more than just a friend to you, Rachel. Do you think we have a chance together? I promise I won't push you. I know now how important it is to keep your identity as it is now. And I'm grateful. Without your memory of being Nora, you wouldn't have known how that water would shoot out of the faucet with such force when you triggered the emergency shower. And without your memory of being Rachel, you wouldn't have known how to clue me in without letting Corrie know what you were planning. It took both sides of you to save the day—to save both of our lives."

"We saved each other, I think." But Rachel felt herself relax. He really did understand. She smiled up at Michael.

He did not smile back. His face still held the granite-hard facade that he had worn that day when she had first confronted him outside the café, the day they first met in Sleepy Cove. But she knew him well enough to recognize that he wasn't hiding anger, not anymore. If he weren't such a self-confident man, she would have thought he looked nervous.

Rachel said, "The last thing I wanted is to make a decision based on fear. But it's true what the Bible says about love driving out fear. I don't want to stay in Sleepy Cove for the rest of my life. I'm going to come back to Eugene, maybe even back to work at the lab if the investors want to keep it going."

Michael still had questions. "Did you really mean that, what you said to Vance in the lab that night? Would you really have given in to his demands just to keep me alive? Let them drug me?"

"Yes." Rachel remembered those last terrifying moments in the lab. Then she let out her breath. "Yes, I would. If it kept you alive to come back to yourself another day."

He started to lift up his hands, as if to put his arms around her, then he hesitated. "I understand you better now. Why you kept pushing away the thought of no longer being Rachel, of losing yourself. I didn't appreciate fully the magnitude of what you were facing until I had to deal with it myself. It is a kind of death."

"That's true. But the love doesn't die. That's what I learned when you found me. No matter what you were telling me, no matter how crazy your story seemed, I wanted to believe it. Because I believe in you." She took a deep breath. After all, the words came easily to her lips. "Because I love you."

He swallowed. "So—if you still remember being Nora…and you're still standing here, talking to me…do you think we could take up where we left off?" She felt the cold touch of metal as he slipped the ring on her finger. "Stop me if I'm going too fast. But I want a life with you, and I don't want to wait. I love you, Rachel. Will you marry me?"

"Of course." He did not move, but his eyes asked questions she did not know how to answer in words. She stood on tiptoe and brushed her lips against his, because she could. Because he was hers and always would be. "But there's just one thing."

"What's that?" His arms came around her and he drew her close, where she belonged. With him.

Rachel looked up at him. The past wasn't so

scary now, and with Michael at her side, there was nothing to fear in her present or future, either. She said, "Call me Nora."

* * * * *

Dear Reader,

Thank you so much for reading *Dangerous Deception*. I hope you enjoyed reading it as much as I did writing it.

In this story, Rachel found that the greatest obstacle she had to overcome was inside her own mind. Sometimes our greatest enemy is fear.

Everyone feels anxious from time to time. An anxiety disorder is a long-term problem that interferes with daily living. If you find fear is holding you back from living your life fully, turning to a doctor or therapist really can help. And a faith in a higher power can give you the strength you need to deal with the problems that you're facing, as well as a peace that passes all understanding.

When the world around you seems dark, there is always One who can help you walk in the light.

If you're curious about how I pictured Rachel and Michael and the settings for *Dangerous Deception*, check out my Pinterest board for this story: https://pin.it/4qBnNAk.

I love hearing from readers! You can write to me c/o Love Inspired, 195 Broadway, 24th floor, New York, NY 10007. I'm still figuring out Facebook, but you can visit me there at https://www.facebook.com/evelynhillauthor.

Or you can always contact me through my website, evelynhillauthor.com.

Blessings,
Evelyn

Get 4 FREE REWARDS!

We'll send you 2 FREE Books plus 2 FREE Mystery Gifts.

Love Inspired books feature uplifting stories where faith helps guide you through life's challenges and discover the promise of a new beginning.

FREE Value Over $20

YES! Please send me 2 FREE Love Inspired Romance novels and my 2 FREE mystery gifts (gifts are worth about $10 retail). After receiving them, if I don't wish to receive any more books, I can return the shipping statement marked "cancel." If I don't cancel, I will receive 6 brand-new novels every month and be billed just $5.24 each for the regular-print edition or $5.99 each for the larger-print edition in the U.S., or $5.74 each for the regular-print edition or $6.24 each for the larger-print edition in Canada. That's a savings of at least 13% off the cover price. It's quite a bargain! Shipping and handling is just 50¢ per book in the U.S. and $1.25 per book in Canada.* I understand that accepting the 2 free books and gifts places me under no obligation to buy anything. I can always return a shipment and cancel at any time. The free books and gifts are mine to keep no matter what I decide.

Choose one: ☐ **Love Inspired Romance Regular-Print**
(105/305 IDN GNWC)

☐ **Love Inspired Romance Larger-Print**
(122/322 IDN GNWC)

Name (please print)

Address   Apt. #

City   State/Province   Zip/Postal Code

Email: Please check this box ☐ if you would like to receive newsletters and promotional emails from Harlequin Enterprises ULC and its affiliates. You can unsubscribe anytime.

Mail to the **Reader Service:**
IN U.S.A.: P.O. Box 1341, Buffalo, NY 14240-8531
IN CANADA: P.O. Box 603, Fort Erie, Ontario L2A 5X3

Want to try 2 free books from another series! Call 1-800-873-8635 or visit www.ReaderService.com.

---

*Terms and prices subject to change without notice. Prices do not include sales taxes, which will be charged (if applicable) based on your state or country of residence. Canadian residents will be charged applicable taxes. Offer not valid in Quebec. This offer is limited to one order per household. Books received may not be as shown. Not valid for current subscribers to Love Inspired Romance books. All orders subject to approval. Credit or debit balances in a customer's account(s) may be offset by any other outstanding balance owed by or to the customer. Please allow 4 to 6 weeks for delivery. Offer available while quantities last.

Your Privacy—Your information is being collected by Harlequin Enterprises ULC, operating as Reader Service. For a complete summary of the information we collect, how we use this information and to whom it is disclosed, please visit our privacy notice located at corporate.harlequin.com/privacy-notice. From time to time we may also exchange your personal information with reputable third parties. If you wish to opt out of this sharing of your personal information, please visit readerservice.com/consumerschoice or call 1-800-873-8635. **Notice to California Residents**—Under California law, you have specific rights to control and access your data. For more information on these rights and how to exercise them, visit corporate.harlequin.com/california-privacy.

LI20R2

THE WESTERN HEARTS COLLECTION!

19 FREE BOOKS in all!

COWBOYS. RANCHERS. RODEO REBELS.
Here are their charming love stories in one prized Collection:
51 emotional and heart-filled romances that capture the majesty and rugged beauty of the American West!

YES! Please send me **The Western Hearts Collection** in Larger Print. This collection begins with 3 FREE books and 2 FREE gifts in the first shipment. Along with my 3 free books, I'll also get the next 4 books from The Western Hearts Collection, in LARGER PRINT, which I may either return and owe nothing, or keep for the low price of $5.45 U.S./$6.23 CDN each plus $2.99 U.S./$7.49 CDN for shipping and handling per shipment*. If I decide to continue, about once a month for 8 months I will get 6 or 7 more books but will only need to pay for 4. That means 2 or 3 books in every shipment will be FREE! If I decide to keep the entire collection, I'll have paid for only 32 books because 19 books are FREE! I understand that accepting the 3 free books and gifts places me under no obligation to buy anything. I can always return a shipment and cancel at any time. My free books and gifts are mine to keep no matter what I decide.

☐ 270 HCN 5354   ☐ 470 HCN 5354

Name (please print)

Address   Apt. #

City   State/Province   Zip/Postal Code

Mail to the **Reader Service:**
IN U.S.A.: P.O. Box 1341, Buffalo, N.Y. 14240-8531
IN CANADA: P.O. Box 603, Fort Erie, Ontario L2A 5X3